The Enlightened Spaniel

The Cat with One Life Left

Gary Heads

Illustrations by Toby Ward

EIGHT NUISANCE
PUBLISHING

First published in Great Britain by Right Nuisance Publishing in 2020

This paperback edition published by Right Nuisance Publishing in 2020
Right Nuisance Publishing website address is
www.rightnuisancepublishing.com

Illustrations by Toby Ward

A CIP catalogue record for this book
is available from the British Library

ISBN paperback 978-1-9164468-2-3
ISBN ebook 978-1-9164468-3-0

Also by Gary Heads

The Enlightened Spaniel – One Dog's Quest to be a
Buddhist

Three things cannot be long hidden: the sun, the moon, and the truth.

Do not dwell in the past, do not dream of the future, concentrate the mind on the present moment. All that we are is the result of what we have thought. We are what we think. All that we are arises with our thoughts.

With our thoughts, we make the world. The mind is everything.

What you think you become.

You, yourself, as much as anybody in the entire universe, deserve your love and affection. We are shaped by our thoughts; we become what we think. When the mind is pure, joy follows like a shadow that never leaves.

Health is the greatest gift, contentment the greatest wealth, faithfulness the best relationship. Peace comes from within. Do not seek it without.

Thousands of candles can be lighted from a single candle, and the life of the candle will not be shortened. Happiness never decreases by being shared.

Buddha

For my grandchildren
Kelsey, Cade, Emily, and Asher

CONTENTS

The Path to Enlightenment – One Year On

1

An Unexpected Visitor

17

Impermanence –the tale of the wobbly tooth

28

Tiny Steps around the River

44

The Phenomena called Jessica

57

The Moggy Meditation Group are Revolting

72

My Monastery is bigger than your Monastery

82

A Trip to the Countryside – anxiety goes on holiday

92

The Buddha's Footsteps, Suspicious Minds, and
Prayer Flags in the Wind

114

Wandering Mind – and the shadow of Fear

125

Do Cats Actually have Nine Lives? – a ginger mishap

138

The Bookshelf's Theory

144

The Truth is Revealed

165

The Leaving

173

1

The Path to Enlightenment – One Year On

Time. Like a petal in the wind, Flows softly by. As old lives are taken, New ones begin. A continual chain, Which lasts throughout eternity. Every life but a minute in time, But each of equal importance.

Cindy Cheney

Once we have crossed the bridge, it's full steam ahead and up the steps of The Leafy Path.

IT IS EXACTLY ONE year since Half-Sister made the monumental decision to dedicate her spaniel life to following the teachings of the Buddha - how time flies! Therefore, it goes without saying that we are all one year older. Apart from The Bookshelf that is. He appears to have no interest in the passing of time. He always looks the same to us. Occasionally he gathers a bit of dust, and the ornaments Mum places on his head may change now and again, but, in general, he remains the fountain of knowledge that has never let us down on the path to enlightenment. It wouldn't surprise us if he was the last man standing at the end of time (we think the Amazon man might come a close second).

Throughout the year we have diligently followed the Buddha's teachings, and continue to do our best to put them into practice. Under the bamboo in the back garden remains our chosen place for reflection. The bamboo, however, has grown, and apart from casting an even bigger shadow over the garden, it now provides complete shelter from the rain. The Buddha's statue that Dad carefully positioned at the base of the bamboo has also changed. Over the year it has acquired some splendid green moss. We think it makes the Buddha look rather distinguished, and its presence has attracted an abundance of tiny birds who delight in taking turns to sit on his head. We would hazard a guess that he is unbothered by this feathery development.

The Bookshelf, having taken it upon himself to unravel the workings of Karma and reincarnation, has yet to make any progress regarding Half-Sister's premonition that she is the reincarnation of the Buddha's dog, Right Nuisance. Half-Sister is convinced that she is, and has suggested to The Bookshelf on many occasions that there is no need for further research. That will not stop him - once on a mission, he will not rest until he has the answer. Regardless of what Half-Sister says in public, we know she dreams of one day having the official stamp of approval.

As far as the moggy meditation group is concerned, there is no doubt in their minds that Half-Sister has connections to the Buddha. They hang on her every word, and practice their meditation as if their lives depend upon it. In the past year, with Half-Sister's guidance, they have been transformed from a bunch of street-fighting assassins into a fully-fledged Buddhist sangha. Although every cat within the group is of equal standing, The Ginger One Next Door definitely has his sights firmly set on attaining the position of Half-Sister's assistant. I am not sure he is up to holding down such a responsible position. Just the other day she suggested that, with more effort, he could take his meditation practice to a higher level; since then, he has taken to meditating on car bonnets. He is perhaps not the sharpest pencil in the box, and is potentially one sandwich short of a picnic.

It was on last year's holiday in Scotland (a silent retreat) that revelations began to arise in the mind of Half-Sister. She was never quite the same after that. The experience of spending so much time in nature has worked its magic, and we now have our very own holiday

3

home in the heart of Northumberland. Well, Mum and Dad bought it, but as everyone knows, everything belongs to springer spaniels. Now we can have a silent retreat whenever the mood take us, and embark on long walks in the countryside. Good Karma all round. At our new abode, we even have a ruined castle just around the corner! It has trees growing out of the windows and the roof, and it casts a spooky shadow in the moonlight on our late night saunter.

We do, however, feel a little guilty leaving The Bookshelf behind, as we are sure he would love it here. He assures us that he is fine, and passes the hours reading about Benjamin Franklin, who started the Library Company in 1731. Half-Sister hopes he's not lonely.

Last year's surprise visit to the Buddhist monastery has yet to be repeated. On that day, Half-Sister's decision to creep into the Dhamma Hall and join in with the Evening Puja turned out to be the defining moment in her decision to follow the Buddha's teachings. We are eager to revisit this wonderful place and have the opportunity to meditate and chant with the resident monks and participants. Wandering Mind still talks enthusiastically about the whole experience, especially the part where she harmonised with Half-Sister in the chanting, and took notes. I missed out that day as I was busy being a decoy. It was my distraction technique that enabled Half-Sister to sneak out un-noticed. The nice lady who looked after us never suspected a thing (thanks to my fine decoyness). Next time, things will be different. We have no idea when Dad will decide to take us to the monastery again, but we know he will one day. Until that fateful day arrives, we are simply biding our time. Apart from the occasional anticipation induced spin.

Once again, I have been entrusted with narrating the ongoing story. I must have done a half-decent job on the last one. Either that, or nobody else wants the job. So, here we go....

The dawning of a new day is heralded, as usual, by the click of the central heating waking up. Or, as it is referred to by Half-Sister, the springer spaniel activation system. Half-Sister is very attuned to sound; on car journeys she can navigate by listening to the indicators clicking on and off. She can work out where we are going by how often they activate. A lesson in indicator awareness was kindly offered, but as I am yet to get past the chuffing and panting stage, the offer was politely declined. Soon, the radiators are bursting into life. It's 7.00am, and a warm glow is spreading throughout the house. Looking out of the living room window, I can see the sun rising over the trees that lie just beyond the fence surrounding the back garden. The fence could be described as a work of art; if it lived in a gallery, it might be entitled 'Unfinished Business.' This is not a reflection on Dad's painting skills, more the fact that he has only painted a bit of it. Half-Sister thinks it's cutting edge. I think Dad needs a trip to the DIY store. Said fence is favoured by the local cats, who like to wander along, perusing their domain. They think they look cool strutting their stuff, but actually they look like Long John Silver from Treasure

Island, with two legs on top of the fence and the other two lower down. This is in stark contrast to the squirrels, who leg it along lickety-split.

The rising sun has now reached the point where it is casting shadows that are weaving their way through the leaves of the bamboo, creating intricate patterns on the statue of the Buddha that is positioned underneath. We think this act of natural creativity makes our place of refection look rather pretty. As the sun sweeps its way through the garden and into the house, the dining room slowly becomes brighter. It's as if Mum is in there with her yellow duster and polish - the only difference is that things are happening a bit faster. The sedate nature of Mum's cleaning is mainly due to the fact that she can get distracted by text messages and then forget what she is doing. It is not unusual to find the duster and polish cuddling each other and looking confused on the dining room table. In a similar manner, the vacuum cleaner can often be found standing at the top of the stairs, totally mystified as to what he should be doing, or how he actually got there in the first place.

Eventually, the rays of sunshine reach the domain of The Bookshelf, and he stirs into action. Sleepily, he turns a blank page to greet the new day. I am currently the only one awake to witness this unfolding spectacle, although Half-Sister will have one eye open due to her central heating alarm clock. This is the advantage of sleeping downstairs on the rocky chair in the kitchen - every morning I watch nature start the day with a flourish. Sometimes sunshine, sometimes wind and rain, and if I am lucky, tiny flakes of snow. Everyone that resides upstairs is still snoozing, and has therefore missed the boat. That was a metaphor by the way. I have to thank The Bookshelf for that one; it was his expertise that taught me how drop them in for effect. Anyway, my high-pitched breakfast howl will soon have the house bursting with life. All bets have been suspended as to who will be first down the stairs.

After breakfast it's time to discuss an element of the Buddha's teachings. This splendid ritual has occurred every day since Half-Sister returned from the Buddhist monastery all those months ago. It is The Bookshelf who usually decides the subject, and today is no exception. In his wisdom, he has chosen impermanence. Half-Sister suggests that as this is such a big subject, it might take us all week to even scratch the surface. Unperturbed, The Bookshelf scans through his ever-growing collection of what the Buddha said. Eventually he makes his choice, and we are ready to begin. The first excerpt read out by The Bookshelf is that the Buddha taught that all com-pounded things are impermanent. Anything that can be divided into parts is impermanent. In other words, everything. Thereafter follows a period of silence and reflection (or maybe non-plussedness might be a better description). After a while Half-Sister nods at The Bookshelf, which is the signal that she concurs with his findings. Everything is impermanent, including us. Before The Bookshelf continues his exploration of impermanence, I grab my blanket and a pawful of treats. I might be an impermanent, but as least I will be a warm and munchy one. Following the short comfort break, The Bookshelf cracks on. In his very first sermon after he became enlightened, the Buddha laid out a proposition. He said life is dukkha. Now dukkha is a strange word. It's another one of those Pali words we keep coming across. The Bookshelf has translated many a Pali word for us using Dad's 'Teach Yourself Pali' book. As Pali was the language in the time of the Buddha, we are sure he will be deciphering many more. However, this is a tricky one to translate into English. There is no precise translation, but *stressful*, *unsatisfactory*, and *suffering*, all come close. Apparently, the majority of human beings see themselves as permanent rather than impermanent therefore, separate from everything else. The Buddha said they were ignorant to the true nature of reality. I'm sure he said that in a nice way. I have to say that so far, The Bookshelf's discussion on impermanence has not exactly been a barrel of laughs. Still, it's got time to cheer up. After a tut-tut and a quick flash of the eyes from Half-Sister, the discussion rolls on. Evidently ignorance is the first of something called 'the three poisons', the other two being greed and hate. That's interesting - I was always under the impression that the three poisons were chocolate, raisins and garlic. The Bookshelf continues reading from the Buddha's book and informs us that attaching to things and wanting them to last forever makes us sad and depressed. I know what he means; my paw is empty of treats already. It is wisdom that will show us that the belief that we are separate from everything, is in fact, an illusion. The reliance on things being somehow permanent is a fallacy - it is only by perceiving impermanence that the key to happiness is revealed. By practising The Noble Eightfold Path, we can realise the truth and be free of the three poisons. So endeth today's discussion. I will reflect on that little lot under the bamboo with Half-Sister later. I always ask her opinion, just in case I miss something important. She always seems to get a handle on the Buddha's teachings and has the patience of a saint. Just as well, as I keep asking her to explain things again and again. The Bookshelf is always happy to re-read the Buddha's teachings, but it is only Half-Sister that can find a simple way to explain a complicated subject.

One of the first things Half-Sister taught me on the path to enlightenment was how to practise living in the present moment. She often reminds me that worrying about the past, or trying to predict the future, is a complete waste of my spaniel energy. Now is all there is. With that wisdom ringing in my dangly ears, I head out into the back garden to see who is knocking about. The back garden is big, and ideal for contemplating the wonders of nature (or if the need arises, getting a bout of the zoomies out of your system). As the garden is next to the woods, you never quite know what woodland creature might turn up. Today, however, things are quiet, apart from two wood pigeons who are sitting next to each other on the fence. So as to remain undetected, I sneak through the bushes and find an observational spot beneath the bamboo to peruse the aforementioned flying objects. I remember to instigate the mindfulness attitude

of beginner's mind, which for the uninitiated is looking at things as if for the very first time. I highly recommend it. So many times I have discovered that things are not quite as they first appear to be. My initial observation is that wood pigeons are big guys. In fact so big, that it's surprising they can actually fly at all! I love the way they plump up their chests and make themselves look even bigger. I am just getting into full exploratory mode when I am joined by Wandering Mind. She asks very politely if she can join me in the wood pigeon meditation. Why not. She will anyway. I re-focus my attention, and once more bring forth the curious mind, before moving on to exploring the many coloured feathers of the Columba Palumbus (to give it its scientific name). I have to say that on close inspection, they are rather spectacular birds.

I am totally engrossed in wood pigeon plumage when,

all of a sudden, one lets rip with a 'coo roo-c'too-coo' (or something to that effect). The other one answers, and before you know it we have a full-blown conversation going on.

Now, the thing you have to watch out for with Wandering Mind is distraction. She is so adept at the art that she can create more diversions than the council road workers. Once distracted, you can find yourself taking all kinds of unskilful action. Today is a classic example. It all begins innocently enough, with Wandering Mind suggesting that the wood pigeons look like two jumbo jets contemplating whether they have enough fuel to take off. The mental image that arises from that sentence transports us immediately into uncontrollable fits of laughter. In the time it takes to do a quick spin, I find myself testing the wood pigeon aviation theory by charging across the garden to scatt them off the fence. Instinctively, they swoop down into the garden before bouncing a few times off the grassy surface. With their little legs going fifty to the dozen, they eventually manage to get some momentum going. It's touch and go for a moment, but slowly they begin to rise into the air and fly off into the wide blue yonder. Wandering Mind is beside herself, unable to speak for laughing, whilst yours truly is simply racked with guilt. With head lowered I slink into the kitchen, thankful that Half-Sister is not watching, (at least I hope she isn't). Wandering Mind shows no signs of remorse, imagining that if they were real jumbo jets, the passengers would be requesting a stop-off at an underwear shop. For over a year, Half-

Sister has been encouraging me to practise my meditation every day. She says mindfulness is the gatekeeper of the mind. Trouble is, I keep losing the key.

Following Half-Sister's meditation practice, it's time for a walk with Dad. There are a lot of splendid walks where we live, but on weekdays we usually take a trip around the river and up the leafy path. That's fine by us - we like that walk. It also gives us an opportunity to meet our pals, both human and otherwise. Which ever way you decide to walk, it's either up a big hill or down a big hill. As Mum has a habit of giving things names (both people and inanimate objects), we go down Cardiac Hill, and up The Leafy Path. In keeping with Mum's naming ritual the first person we meet on today's walk is Mrs Bobble Hat. Now Mrs Bobble Hat probably has no idea that this is her name. However, if you wear a bright yellow bobble hat all year round, it should perhaps come as no surprise. She lives down by the river with her West Highland terrier. He doesn't have a bobble hat, but can sometimes be seen out wearing his tartan jacket. Lucky escape that one.

When we get to the bottom of the hill, we turn left and begin walking the length of the river as far as the little green bridge. On the way, we will pass both the local bakery and the community centre. Half-Sister's nose is always twitching *way* before the bakery ever comes into sight. Now, as with most things connected to food, Half-Sister has a history. Usually there is a cunning plan, and an associated tale that ends up in spaniel folklore.

The bakery is no exception. For all those dogs reading this with their owners and considering adapting Half-Sister's blueprint to suit their own circumstances, please take note of the following: there are certain ingredients required before Half-Sister's cunning plan will work like clockwork. In our case, it needs to be Monday and a sunny day. Monday is roast beef dinner day for the local pensioners, who just happen to be ingredient number three. The sunny day is an *essential* requirement, as this encourages the pensioners to sit outside to eat their dinner. The final ingredient is Half-Sister's 'help me I'm starving' expression, and bingo! Dinner is served. All that is left are empty plates and a variety of pensioners counting their fingers. It is not that Half-Sister takes anything that is not being offered, but rather that the speed at which the roast dinner disappears is too much for your average pensioner to comprehend. Today, much to Half-Sister's disappointment, there is not a pensioner in sight. The only thing of note is a sign in the bakery window informing us that there are no pies left.

Continuing on, we arrive at the building known to the local residents as the community centre. You can hardly see inside the windows for all the posters detailing forthcoming events. Today, the building is a hive of activity due to it being slimming club day. Because of this popular event, we have to cross the road and walk a while on the grassy bank. It is not so much the number of cars parked along the road that is causing the issue, but more the rotund nature of the participants who are wobbling towards the entrance. It does not take a genius to work out today's bakery sign.

In the very next breath, I find myself sitting on the grassy bank being lectured by Half-Sister. Said lecture is all about non-judgemental thinking. Wandering Mind is also subject to a ticking-off for her input. We take Half-Sister's words on board, and promise to mend our ways. I am sure in a few weeks' time the slimming club members will strut out of the community centre looking like stick insects (another lecture from Half-Sister).

If the embarrassment of a dressing down in public was not enough, she then proceeds to give us homework. This is not the first time we have been reprimanded by Half-Sister and issued with an assignment to emphasis the point. It is The Bookshelf who usually oversees our progress, and there is no messing with him. For our misdemeanours we have to memorize the following and complete the exercise below every day.

Non-Judging - *Being an impartial witness of your own experience requires that you become aware of the constant stream of judging and reacting to inner and outer experiences that we are normally caught up in, observe it, and step back from it. Just observe how much you are preoccupied with liking and disliking during a ten-minute period as you go about your business.*

Wandering Mind volunteers to be the impartial witness and has gone to get her swimming costume so she can sit in the stream of judging and reacting. Half-Sister shakes her head, and the walk continues. I am not sure Wandering Mind's last comment was a wise one. In fact, I know it wasn't.

With our ticking-off over (for now), the little green bridge looms large. It's made of girders like Irn Bru, and has gaps that allow you to see the river flowing under-neath. It is just big enough for people to pass, however two people with dogs is a risk many avoid. Therefore, there is an unwritten rule that you wait if somebody is already crossing with their dog. The bridge holds the distinction of being in Tyne & Wear when you start to cross, and County Durham when you get to the other side. Or vice versa, depending on which way you are walking. Once we have crossed the bridge, it's full steam ahead and up the steps of The Leafy Path. After navigating the uneven steps, we reach the main road. It's plain sailing from now on as we pass the human vets on the other side of the road and head back home. Unless Half-Sister decides to introduce herself to everyone at the bus stop, we will be back at our house in a matter of minutes. The Bookshelf would tell you exactly what this beautiful area of countryside is called. In fact, he would give you the grid reference, and the area's local history if you asked him. We are just happy to call it home.

2

An Unexpected Visitor

"I love the outdoors and looking at snakes, squirrels, bugs - just going through the woods and being part of it. You can smell the different trees. And I listen. There's so much you can learn by listening, by sitting and watching things happen".

Boo Weekley

Half-Sister has just finished her opening chant, when all of a sudden the group dispense with their dignified postures and are up on their toes with arched backs.

TODAY BEGINS LIKE ANY other day. A leisurely trip around the back garden, followed by breakfast, which is served on time and duly disappears at the speed of light. In fact, this particular day portrays all the hallmarks of business as usual. It provides no hint of it being a monumental day in the lives of yours truly and Half-Sister. In the dining room, The Bookshelf begins to stir from his slumber. He flicks through a page or two, more from habit than study. He's always been a late riser, but burns the midnight oil if he finds something of interest, which he does on most days.

Today is Monday, and the beginning of a new week for our human pals, although it is just another day to us. As is her inclination, Half-Sister has asked The Bookshelf where the word Monday originates from. After a quick ponder, he informs us that it was named after the Old English word for moon. In Latin, moon is Luna, That might not give us Monday, but it does give us the words lunar, lunatic, and lunacy. Half-Sister considers this carefully and then declares that it all makes sense. If you create a seven-day week and then work five of them, lunatic and lunacy are just perfect.

Monday aside, today is meditation practice day for the local cats, guided as usual by Half-Sister. We can see through the lounge window that they are starting to arrive. The Ginger One Next Door is first; this is due to a combination of eagerness and the fact that he lives next door. He is the original member of the moggy meditation group and therefore has the longest established practice. In fact, in the beginning, he benefitted from one-to-one sessions. You could say he was Half-Sister's ginger guinea pig. We think he sees himself as some kind of moggy monastic - he has a habit of positioning himself right next to Half-Sister, and is always the last one to leave. The Ginger One is swiftly followed by his shadow, The Siamese from across the road, although that statement is debatable. The Siamese treats The Ginger One's house like the local Airbnb - he is not adverse to eating his tea, or cosying up in his favourite spot. Due to The Ginger One currently practising loving-kindness meditation, The Siamese gets away with it. For now. Half-Sister was unsure about The Siamese when he first arrived on the scene. Her usual ploy of planting her eyeballs straight at you and weighing you up produced very little in the case of The Siamese. This was mainly down to him having eyeballs that go in a variety of directions. This strange phenomena was referred to The Bookshelf for further clarification; it seems The Siamese has an interesting history to say the least. For starters, he originates from Thailand (formally known as Siam, hence his name). How he made it to the Western world remains a mystery - a bit like how he just turns up in The Ginger One's house. There is a whole host of legends concerning how he got his dodgy peepers, not to mention his crooked tail. It is believed that Siamese cats once lived in monasteries and temples and were often entrusted with guarding valuable possessions, like vases. They would curl their tails around the vase and stare at it until they went cross-eyed. Looking at the evidence, Half-Sister is far from convinced this legend is factual. She is wondering about the Lasa Apso dog that was renowned for guarding monasteries. He wouldn't have taken kindly to a cross-eyed, curly tailed moggy muscling in on his patch. Then there is the issue of Siamese cats being very talkative. This would not have been helpful towards creating a peaceful atmosphere in the monastery for meditation practice. Weighing up the facts, the only one Half-Sister is prepared to give any credence to is the cross-eyed bit. This is based on the fact that she has noticed she can go cross-eyed staring at her empty food bowl at five-o-clock waiting for tea. You can't argue with science.

Next to arrive is The White One with a tiny black bit and the very end of his tail. Another tomcat, and perhaps the oldest kid on the block. After months of attending the moggy meditation group, he has finally learnt to accept that the black bit at the end of his tail is just the way things are. This is progress, as he used to have sleepless nights worrying that Half-Sister's playful suggestion that he was a dodgy reincarnation of a black cat might be true. Eventually, the group is augmented by The Wheezy Twins, two asthmatic, steroid-pumped male cats from across the road. We are not insinuating that they visit the vets often; however, Half-Sister has suggested that it would be appropriate for The Wheezy Twins to have their names displayed on the vets shiny new top-of-the-range BMW. Everyone is present and correct, and already beginning to take up their dignified postures in anticipation of today's session.

It's cold outside, and there is a powdery mist drifting

into the garden. All this ghostly weather is making the Buddha and the bamboo appear atmospheric, rather like a film set from a horror movie. The Bookshelf and I are happy to watch through the dining room window, ably assisted by the radiator. Half-Sister has just finished her opening chant, when all of a sudden the group dispense with their dignified postures and are up on their toes with arched backs. Something is approaching through the mist. Now, it is not uncommon for the occasional stray cat to stumble upon the moggy meditation group. The fence is a well-travelled highway for cats that choose to journey through the woods. Usually they are welcomed with open arms and invited to participate - some do, some don't. However, there is something very different about today's visitor, and the group are wary to say the least. Half-Sister is never fazed by the arrival of a cat, but we can all see the impact this unexpected guest is having on everyone else. All of a sudden the mist evaporates, and there he is. It is obvious to us that he is a tomcat, and a big one at that. Now, unlike the dodgy peepers belonging to The Siamese, this guy appears to have one eye in perfect working order, and the other one in need of some attention. The good eye is a striking gold colour, but the other one is clouded and dull. He approaches the group slowly; The Bookshelf thinks he walks like John Wayne, whoever he is. You can tell that at one time his coat would have been strikingly black; now it seems to consist of every pantone reference to grey. He is lean, bordering on skinny, and looks like an old jigsaw with several pieces missing. His ears look like bus tickets that

21

have been clipped by the conductor. He has made a lot of journeys. There are whiskers missing, and a half-moon scar stretches itself across his shiny black nose. His trajectory is unmistakably towards the group - it's like watching a Theravadin monk immersed in a walking meditation; focused, and only mindful of the next step. When he gets close enough, Half-Sister asks if he would like to join them. He nods his head as a sign of acceptance, and takes up a remarkably good dignified posture. The moggy meditation group, realising that he is not just passing through, shuffle around and make room for their unexpected visitor. They just smile at him, which seems the safest bet. The Bookshelf, who has been watching proceedings through the dining room window, begins to draw up a contract for the transference of territorial rights for The Ginger One Next Door, or anyone else for that matter. He is not expecting a legal challenge.

Half-Sister begins by guiding a sitting meditation. The new arrival sits in his dignified posture like a statue. His eyes are tight shut, and there is an air of confidence about him that suggests he knows he is perfectly safe to sit in this manner. This is in stark contrast to the other members of the group who seem to have transported themselves to the local disco and are currently engaged in a shuffle. The Bookshelf is confused by this description, and so looks up the meaning of the word shuffle.

To move your feet or bottom around while staying in the same place, especially because you are uncomfortable, nervous or embarrassed.

That is all true, but he omitted to include dancing.

We should just have asked Dad, as he is the master of the shuffle. We hope he never reads this book.

When the sitting meditation is completed, everyone slowly opens their eyes and prepares for Half-Sister's dharma talk. All apart from the latest member that is; he remains in his dignified posture and still has his eyes closed. Seeing the uneasiness that has spread through the group, Half-Sister dispenses with her original topic for the dharma talk, and instead chooses acceptance. Hopefully this will settle everyone down, especially The Wheezy Twins. Their breathing has now reached volcanic proportions, and the rolls of fat on their tiny bodies are going up and down faster than an accordion at a ce'ilidh. The Ginger One and The Siamese, meanwhile, are still in smiling lockdown, even though the beneficiary of their grimace has his eyes shut. The White One is playing safe and pretending to hypnotize his tail. Throughout Half-Sister's dharma talk, the unexpected visitor does not move a muscle, or even open his eyes once. Despite this, Half-Sister's intuition is telling her that he is listening intently. As soon as the session ends, the group disperses at speed. The Bookshelf, who we do not doubt in these matters, reckons that the domestic cat has a top speed of 30mph over a short distance. That could be an underestimate.

All that remains is Half-Sister and the dodgy-eyed black one, surrounded by a cloud of moggy-induced dust. He is still sitting in his rather perfect dignified posture, but now has his eyes open. Half-Sister begins a gentle enquiry to ascertain just who this mysterious guest is. Turns out his name is Amara. Interesting name that one, sounds a bit antediluvian to me. Anyway, I like it. It definitely sounds more mystical than The Ginger One Next Door, who is currently hiding under the bed. The Bookshelf is intrigued by the name Amara, and is searching for a definition (this is after he reminds me of what antediluvian-*ancient*-means).

It turns out that Amara wandering into the back garden and dropping in on the moggy meditation group was no accident. He has been searching for months to locate the whereabouts of Half-Sister. He tells her that her reputation as a skilful teacher, and for the wisdom she imparts, has spread far and wide. Way beyond the end of the street, and further than the leafy path, apparently. Who would have thought it?

After a long conversation, Half-Sister finally returns to the house. The Bookshelf and I can hardly contain our eagerness to get the lowdown on Amara. Evidently, our mysterious visitor is not the tough guy that his appearance suggests, although we think he has been formidable in the past. His long trek to seek out the wise spaniel called Half-Sister is due to him being wracked with anxiety. She is his last hope. The Bookshelf enquires into just what Amara is so anxious about. He is intrigued that such a strong and fearsome cat has been reduced to such a state. Half-Sister settles in and shifts into storytelling mode - we like it when she does this. As we suspected, Amara has indeed lived an interesting life. In fact, he has travelled far and wide. Unlike us, he has had several owners and has lived in many cities around the world. He once lived with a beggar in Calcutta in India, and had to shed fur because of the heat. In Hinduism, the cat is not exactly flavour of the month. If a cat crosses a person's path while they are walking, it is considered bad luck. Equally, if you see a cat when you first wake up you are destined for a bad day. If you happen to kill a cat, it is viewed as extremely sinful and you will incur a whole bucket-full of negative Karma, not to mention offending Shashti Devi, the female god of fertility. To top it off, if a black cat crosses your path before you set off on a journey, you might consider staying in and watching the television instead. Needless to say, nobody bothered Amara in his time in Calcutta.

He then stayed with a family in Genhe, Inner Mongolia, and had to grow a thick coat as it's one of the coldest places on Earth. Although the winters were long and the summers short, it was whilst living in Genhe that Amara witnessed what he considers to be a Wonder of the World. One day, an apparition made it appear that there were three suns on the horizon. The middle one was the actual sun, and the other two were smaller reflections. This is known as an *anthelion* - an optical phenomenon caused by the sun high in the sky shining through hexagonal snow crystals in the air. This is all fascinating stuff, but also expensive, as The Bookshelf already has a list as long as his shelf for the Amazon man.

Amara eventually ended up in Tibet, where he was taken in by a friendly monk. He liked it there but had to leave unexpectedly. Due to circumstances beyond his control he ended up as a rat catcher on a ship, and was nearly washed overboard in a gigantic storm. Now he is in our back garden, obviously via the scenic route. An adventurous life like Amara's doesn't come without a certain degree of risk and potential danger. On many occasions he has thought his time was up, only to avoid the inevitable by the skin of his teeth. He had lived a life blessed with good fortune, but deep down there was a nagging feeling of uneasiness beginning to arise.

One thing the Tibetan monk had taught Amara was how to meditate; he has practised ever since. The Bookshelf and I share a lightbulb moment - so that's where the dignified posture comes from! Sitting in the monastery garden one day, he began to recall all the dodgy situations he had just managed to avoid. Amara reflected upon the ancient myth that cats have nine lives. Reluctantly, he started to count the lives he had potentially lost to adversity. It was at that precise moment that the anxiety and panic kicked in. According to his calculations, he only had one life left. A feeling of uneasiness has been with him ever since.

One thing Half-Sister did not discover was how Amara found out about her and the moggy meditation group in the first place. Surely stumbling upon our back garden accidently would fall firmly in the needle and haystack category. Despite the holes in Amara's story, Half-Sister will still do her best to help him overcome his anxiety. He is currently camped out in Dad's new storage box in the garden. Half-Sister reckons Dad will find him in the morning and feed him.

We are just letting everything sink in when The Bookshelf suddenly has a giant wobble. This is a sign he has found something significant, and judging by the size of the wobble, it's a biggy.

He explains to us that he was beginning to think he would find nothing regarding the definition of Amara. This would have been highly unusual, as The Bookshelf is meticulous in his work. Turns out he was simply looking in the wrong place, and hadn't gone back far enough in time. According to the multi-shelved one (to give him his pet name) the Buddha walked through a city in India and stopped to give a talk. To enable people to find him, he left footprints in the sand. The two chiefs of the city followed the Buddha's footprints, and upon listening to his talk they became monks. That city was called Amara. The Bookshelf thought that was it, until he looked in his Sanskrit dictionary. There it was staring him in the wood - the definition of Amara: *undying, immortal, a god*.

Reflections under the bamboo

This evening's reflection under the bamboo is dominated by one subject: Amara. Just who is this mysterious cat, and what is he really doing taking up residence in our back garden? For now, we are giving him the benefit of the doubt and going with the anxiety story. Half-Sister has an open mind on the issue, but I am wary. The Bookshelf is far from convinced, and is continuing his research. The members of the moggy meditation group are currently walking around as if they have robbed the local bank and the police are looking for them. All apart from The Ginger One Next Door, who is still under the bed. There is no sign of Amara.

3

Impermanence – the tale of the wobbly tooth

"Anyone who has lost something they thought was theirs forever finally comes to realise that nothing really belongs to them."

Paulo Coelho

They are all in attendance, including Amara, who winks at me with his dodgy eye as I approach the group.

IT'S A STRANGE COINCIDENCE that just the other day we were talking about impermanence, and this morning Half-Sister announces from the top of the stairs that she has a wobbly front tooth. In fact, she is currently barking with a slight lisp.

According to the Buddha, all that exists is impermanent; nothing lasts. Therefore nothing can be grasped or held onto. If we fail to understand the essence of this teaching then we will inevitably suffer. It seems Half-Sister's tooth was always destined to fall out. Today just happens to be the day. Furthermore, The Bookshelf said there were no coincidences, just synchronicities; two events that come together for a purpose. I wonder what events have conspired to wobble Half-Sister's front gnasher, and more to the point, what is she going to do about it?

Fortunately she doesn't have to do anything about her wobbly tooth, as Dad is quick to spot Half-Sister's wonky smile. After a quick consultation with Mum, a vet's appointment is swiftly booked. In the blink of an eye, she is sitting in the back seat of the car and heading down the street. Just before the car drives away, Mum informs Half-Sister that she isn't to worry, as the Tooth Fairy will be paying her a visit tonight and leaving a treat under her blanket. As Half-Sister has the full complement of forty-two teeth, The Bookshelf and I think it best to hide Dad's pliers. Better safe than sorry.

It is one of Half-Sister's most endearing traits that, as suggested by the Buddha, she questions everything. In her wobbly-induced absence, The Bookshelf and I are carrying on the tradition by inquiring into the whole

Tooth Fairy issue. Interestingly, receiving a reward for placing your tooth under a pillow (or a blanket in Half-Sister's case) dates all the way back to Viking times. Viking warriors would collect their children's baby teeth when they fell out and wear them as a bracelet to help protect them in battle. According to Norse mythology, teeth were also burned or buried to ward off witches and protect people in the afterlife. We are just about to wind up the Tooth Fairy research project when The Bookshelf finds something of significance. After a short pause, he excitedly announces that when the Buddha died (sighs all round), he was cremated. After the cremation, for whatever reason, one of his loyal followers decided to take a tooth from the Buddha's remains. This tooth has been passed down over the years and is now a famous artefact. It is kept in a set of seven golden boxes - a bit like Russian dolls - and there is even a Buddha tooth relic temple. Maybe the vet will give Dad Half-Sister's tooth so we can bury it beside the Buddha under the bamboo. We don't have seven golden boxes, or any Russian dolls for that matter, but we could put it in seven poo bags (clean). Due to being engrossed in fairy and Buddha tooth contemplation, we are surprised to see the sun casting a shadow over the dining room. We stand motionless as the room darkens in front of our eyes; however, it is not the passing of time that has us transfixed, but rather the realization that evening is fast approaching and we are still one Half-Sister missing. To compound things even further, Dad has just returned from the vets, empty-spanieled.

After tea (which was served on time and, for once, was a solitary experience), I settle myself on the sofa. There is plenty of room tonight, and it's quiet without Half-Sister's snoring. Anyone who has ever had a springer spaniel will know that we can fall asleep upside down, with our legs straight, and pointing at the ceiling. This position is complimented by having half our body facing one way, and the other half facing in the other direction. In keeping with the age old spaniel tradition, an emergency yellow tennis ball is wedged behind the back of the head. You never know when it might be needed, and you wouldn't want to get caught short.

As I am two years younger than Half-Sister, this will actually be the first time I have slept in the house without her. The Bookshelf asks me how I feel about being the only dog in the house. I need to reflect upon that one.

Using my mindfulness skills taught to me by Half-Sister I tune into my emotions, feelings, and thoughts. The overriding feeling is a strange one. I would best describe it as a mixture of bricking it, combined with a power surge brought on by being in charge of the house. I decide the wisest thing to do is just have a snooze and let the Universe take care of everything else.

Sometime later I awake to total darkness and the sound of a voice echoing around the living room. For one moment I think it is Half-Sister speaking to me from beyond. However, once I get my bearings I am relieved to recognise the voice as being that of The Bookshelf. Why do people ask if you are asleep? The answer has to be no. If you are awake you will answer; if you are asleep they have just woken you up so you will answer anyway. The untimely interruption is down to The Bookshelf being unable to sleep due to ruminating about Half-Sister not returning from the vets. In addition to the non-returning Half-Sister issue, he has identified a further problem that is causing him to feel apprehensive. In our concern for Half-Sister, we have completely forgotten that tomorrow is moggy meditation day. As their spiritual leader is currently AWOL, it will apparently be down to me to guide the meditation and conduct the dharma talk. Now there are two of us feeling apprehensive. It's not guiding the meditation that fills me with trepidation - I have listened to Half-Sister do that hundreds of times - however, a dharma talk is a whole different ball game. Not being an expert on the Buddha's teachings makes a dharma talk difficult. On top of that, the Buddha could be listening from under the bamboo. The Bookshelf has offered to supply me with notes if I pick a teaching to talk about, but even the thought of it sends shivers down my tail. Maybe Half-Sister will turn up in the morning, or the heavens will open and rain will stop play. I think a period of reflection is needed to consider my options. Tomorrow, I will be heading for the bamboo for some serious dharma talk contemplation.

In the morning, what has been my daily routine for the past six years is completely obliterated by Half-Sister's absence. Without her barking for breakfast at the top of the stairs, I sleep in for the first time ever. This leads to a chain reaction. Without my high-pitched whining at his bedroom door, Dad also sleeps in. All this sleepiness results in breakfast being served late. The Bookshelf, meanwhile, is a flutter of quivering pages. His wandering mind is running amok with potential reasons as to why he is still alone at this hour of the day. Eventually, when I trundle down the stairs, he realises we haven't moved house, and so closes the book on the situation.

After a quick trip round the garden followed by some necessities, I head for the bamboo as previously arranged.

I am just cosying up to the Buddha hoping for divine inspiration when I happen to notice Amara at the base of the bamboo. I can hardly see him, as he is surrounded by bamboo leaves which are hiding his jet-black body. His eyes are blending in with the yellowy green leaves (especially his dodgy one, which is almost the same colour). I think it's scary how he just arrives unannounced - one minute he is nowhere to be seen, and the next minute he is standing right in front of you. It's as if he has teleported in from his alien spacecraft. Half-Sister thinks I have been sitting next to Mum watching Star Trek for too long. Amara enquires about the whereabouts of Half-Sister, so I tell him the tale of the wobbly tooth. I am careful not to give too much information away in case it gets back to the moggy meditation group. However, being the wily old tom cat that he is, he asks me what I am going to discuss in the dharma talk. This is not the first time he has plucked thoughts right out of my head. I need to have a chat with Wandering Mind, as she needs to learn to close the door behind her.

As he seems to have acquired some kind of telepathic ability, I might as well spill the beans about my anxiety over the dharma talk. What harm can it do? He probably knows all about it anyway. I decide to let rip with Half-Sister's expertise being a hard act to follow. After that admission sinks in, I continue the soul-searching by owning up to having a limited knowledge of the Buddha's teachings.

A deep breath later I await Amara's response. No words of wisdom are forthcoming, just a simply reading that I am to think about. Before I can enquire further, he closes his eyes and returns to snooze mode. It seems Half-Sister and I are not the only ones that like to reflect under the bamboo.

I leave him to his slumber and high-tail it to the dining room to recite Amara's quote to The Bookshelf before I forget it –

"By being yourself you put something wonderful in the world that was not there before"

Edwin Elliot

The Bookshelf, intrigued by Amara's wisdom, looks up the quote to see if he can glean further information. After a short while he does his best to explain the meaning behind it, and the potential action I might take. It appears that Amara is hinting at authenticity. Just to back up his findings, The Bookshelf adds his own definition, and tells me Amara is encouraging me to be true to my own personality, spirit and character. In other words, he is telling me to be myself, and that there is no need to copy Half-Sister. I should forget all about those thoughts of self-doubt and just be my true self. See - he is reading my mind again. I instruct The Bookshelf that I will not be needing his notes, although the offer was a very kind one, and that I am off to prepare for my dharma talk.

Later that morning, much to my disappointment, there is still is no sign of Half-Sister. So, notes in paw, I head for the back garden to guide today's moggy meditation class. They are all in attendance, including Amara, who winks at me with his dodgy eye as I approach the group. The Ginger One Next Door looks at me gingerly (what a surprise). The expression on his face suggests he was expecting the meditation wizard, but got the sorcerer's apprentice instead. Meanwhile, The Siamese lets out a long sigh and twirls his crooked tail in annoyance. It appears to me that The Wheezy Twins are breathing twice as fast as normal, their steroid-induced fatness wobbling with the increased motion. Let's hope today is not the day their medication gets the better of them. The only one that seems unperturbed by Half-Sister's absence is The White One. He is simply staring at the black bit at the end of his tail as usual. Ignoring their feline idiosyncrasies, I crack on. I begin the session with the chant Half-Sister brought back from her visit to the monastery last year. She always starts the sessions with this, and repeats it three times.

Namô Tassa Bhagavatô Arahatô Samma Sambuddhassa
Namô Tassa Bhagavatô Arahatô Samma Sambuddhassa
Namô Tassa Bhagavatô Arahatô Samma Sambuddhassa

I remember it took The Bookshelf and I months to find out what she was on about. Eventually, after much persuasion, Wandering Mind cracked, spilling the beans as to the meaning of the ancient words. Fortunately Half-Sister has not found out about our interrogation, or the use of the above metaphor. No doubt she would be asking us what benefit there is to emptying beans in a cross-examination.

I pay homage to the Blessed One, the Perfected One, the
fully Enlightened One.

The chanting seems to have settled them down a little bit. Perhaps the occasional thought has entered their heads that I might know what I am doing. They can file those in the section marked dubious. I encourage them to take a dignified posture using the Buddha under the bamboo as reference - a useful shortcut that one. After much shuffling and adjusting they seem to be ready for today's guided meditation.

As suggested by The Bookshelf, I am keeping things simple: a body and breath meditation should suffice. Half-Sister once told me that a meditation teacher guides participants from their own experience of engaging with the practice. With this in mind, I settle into my best dignified posture and begin exploring how my body feels in this moment. I encourage the moggy meditation group to do the same. To be honest, I sound a bit like a football commentator describing the match on TV. Let's hope I don't score an own goal or give away a penalty. Everything is going swimmingly, when who should arrive on the scene but Wandering Mind. Inevitable.

After her usual antics of placing umpteen thoughts in my head regarding self-doubt, incompetence, Half-Sister's wrath, moggies at the vet's suffering from trauma and insurance claims, she surprisingly offers to be my assistant. Better to have her onside than at her disruptive best, so I agree.

Following a suitable period of bodily exploration, it's now time to move on to the breath. I gently instruct the group to be with their in-breath from the beginning to the end, and then their out-breath from the beginning to the end. It's simple really - just keep breathing and notice all the sensations the breath creates. If you happen to get distracted by Wandering Mind and find yourself lost in thought, just return your attention to the breath when you notice. At this point, Wandering Mind does a little jig of delight at getting a mention, and then tells me to remind them again, and again, and again. This could be the longest ten minute meditation in the history of meditations. Eventually time is up, much to the disappointment of Wandering Mind. It is, however, a relief for The Wheezy Twins, who were visibly wilting near the end.

They all open their eyes and settle down in anticipation of the customary dharma talk. The Siamese uncurls his dignified posture and looks me straight in the eye. Well, I think he does - it's hard to tell with those weird multi-directional peepers. The Ginger One continues his disapproving stare, and The Wheezy Twins sink into the soil like asthmatic playdoh. Unsurprisingly, The White One returns to trying to remove the black bit at the end of his tail using psychokinesis.

Before I begin to speak, Wandering Mind asks me in a whispery voice what my dharma talk is all about. When I tell her, she goes very quiet and reflective. I can just make out her last word as she awaits my talk with great interest. "Really?".

The wise sage returns

Later that afternoon, we are all delighted to witness the return of Half-Sister. According to Dad she is missing not one tooth, but two, and has also had a fatty lump removed from the back of her leg that nobody knew she had. However, we are unable to instigate an interrogation regarding her experience at the vets because Half-Sister appears to be as wobbly as her tooth was before she went to the vets in the first place.

The fact that Half-Sister has ignored her supper, and has instead headed to the sofa, tells us that it would be best to leave things until the morning. The Bookshelf digs out a book on conflict resolution just in case things have not improved by the morning. I decide to inhabit the other sofa and keep a decidedly low profile. Half-Sister is already snoring, and completely oblivious to the fact that there are two treats under her blanket.

Sometimes in life all that is needed for a quick recovery is your own bed and a good kip. So it proves to be the case for Half-Sister, as the following morning she stands at the top of the stairs and barks for her breakfast, albeit with a temporary speech impediment. It turns out that being slightly dodgy in the health department pays dividends as Half-Sister's breakfast consists of chicken and rice. Mum kindly adds a few dollops of chicken into my bowl so I don't feel left out. Let's hope Half-Sister plays this one out for a while.

Following the swift demolition of breakfast and a quick tour of the garden, Half-Sister is finally ready to explain the chain of events that resulted in her staying the night at the veterinary hospital. She confirms that she did indeed have more than just a wobbly tooth, although she is not sure what else transpired. Half-Sister did hear the vet ask if they should remove the fatty lump, but decided that Dad should stay. After that, everything is a blur. Wandering Mind chips in that although she was there, she can't remember anything either. That's a first. The Bookshelf, who has been most concerned about Half-Sister, tells her about the tooth fairy, and the tale of the Buddha's tooth. Her curiosity is immediately aroused, and in that moment her sore mouth and stitched up leg are completely forgotten.

The current whereabouts of Half-Sister's teeth are unknown. We presume that either Dad has them, or they are still at the vets. This is a disappointment to Half-Sister as she liked the idea of burying them beside the Buddha. One thing that has caused confusion in the mind of

Half-Sister is the fact that we have returned seven unused poo bags to the kitchen. We thought it best to leave that one well alone, although she did ask us if we had been unwell. Maybe the teeth will miraculously turn up one day - if not, there is nothing better than a mystery to build your reputation.

Now that we have ascertained why Half-Sister failed to return home, it's time to update her on the moggy meditation group session from yesterday. To say she is surprised that I guided the meditation and delivered the dharma talk would be the understatement of the year. I have not seen that look since we awoke one day to find the statue of the Buddha in the back garden. I carefully explain to Half-Sister about the chanting, and guiding the body and breath meditation with the assistance of Wandering Mind. She seems to accept that, and appears impressed with our efforts. Finally, she looks me straight in the eye - as only Half-Sister can - and enquires into what I actually spoke about in the dharma talk. I am struggling as to where I should begin when I notice through the window that the moggy meditation group has assembled on the back garden fence. "See for yourself," I reply, suggesting she look out the window. There they all are, balanced carefully on the garden fence. The Ginger One Next Door and The Siamese are discussing aerodynamics. They are very animated, and keep holding their legs out to demonstrate. Meanwhile, The Wheezy Twins are debating whether a steroid injection would make any difference to a flight path; a research paper in the making methinks. The White One listens carefully in-between meditating on his black-tipped tail. He swishes it back and forth to see if any black bits take flight. Amara has one eye open, and is looking straight at Half-Sister. The Bookshelf looks on proudly, as Half-Sister shakes her head in disbelief. I think my dharma talk on yellow tennis balls has been a resounding success.

In the evening, we settle in the dining room with The Bookshelf. Usually this is a time for snoozing and watching the sun go down over the back garden. Occasionally we catch a glimpse of The Ginger One Next Door walking along the fence, or The Siamese heading off into the woods. We are never sure where Amara is; he could be far away, or right under our noses. It's impossible to tell.

Not surprisingly, Half-Sister is in a reflective mood tonight, and has been thinking about impermanence and the present moment. After her latest experience, it seems the Buddha's words are ringing loudly in Half-Sister's ears. She is sad that everything changes and that nothing stays forever, but understands the importance of paying attention to what is happening right now. She tells us that our life is just one moment after another and that we need to embrace change, because everything is impermanent, including us. If we cling to the idea that things are otherwise, we will suffer and become anxious and sad.

We have listened to Half-Sister talk about impermanence on many occasions, but this time is different. She really wanted us to get the message. Impermanence, or *Anicca* to give it its Pali translation, is the first of the three marks of existence. The other two being *Dukkha* (suffering), and *Anatta* (non-self). Where would we be without the 'Learn Yourself Pali' book? The Bookshelf reckons he could order from the menu in a Pali restaurant, if we could find one. Anyway, back to Half-Sister's explanation. All physical and mental events come into being and dissolve. We will let the Buddha have the final word on the matter. Impermanence is inescapable - everything vanishes. Therefore, there is nothing more important than continuing on the path to enlightenment with diligence. Half-Sister nods in approval. We are just about to wrap things up when Wandering Mind decides to have the final say. Whatever *IS* will be *WAS*. Now you can't argue with that.

Half-Sister looks tired, and is starting to close her eyes. Just before she goes to sleep she asks The Bookshelf to find a reading to end the day. I complete my habitual bedtime spin, and settle in for the night. Just before I close my eyes I notice Amara standing at the dining room window. I wonder how long he has been there?

Nothing in the world is permanent, and we're foolish when we ask anything to last, but surely we're still more foolish not to take delight in it while we have it.

Somerset Maugham

Reflections under the bamboo

As the days come and go, Half-Sister continues to recover from her ordeal and is now virtually back to her old self. After a visit to the vets she was passed fit and has now resumed her teaching duties. My career as a meditation teacher has ended - redundant at age six. Still, my efforts have not been wasted, as the moggies can often be seen sitting on the garden fence looking longingly at my tennis ball aerobics. I think they may have found their inner dog. There is still no sign of Half-Sister's teeth, so any thoughts of worship and burial ceremonies have been put on hold. The moggy meditation group seem to have gotten over this one fairly quickly and are currently consoling themselves with thoughts of Wimbledon.

We have all taken Half-Sister's words on impermanence to heart, and are doing our best to live in the present moment. Her explanation has certainly affected The Bookshelf, who is leaving nothing to chance. In the likelihood that both Half-Sister and yours truly go AWOL, he has prepared a dharma talk. He has informed us that it is all about impermanence and is entitled 'Embracing Your Inner Woodworm'. We shall look forward to hearing that one.

4

Tiny Steps around the River

"There is always a step small enough from where we are to get us to where we want to be. If we take that small step, there's always another we can take, and eventually a goal thought to be too far to reach becomes achievable".

Ellen Langer

Standing in front of our eyes are the fattest pair of spaniels you have ever seen.

AS HALF-SISTER PREDICTED, DAD found our mysterious visitor sleeping in his new garden storage box. After recovering from the initial shock, Amara was duly fed, and an order for cat food placed and delivered, much to the surprise of the Amazon man. He now spends his days either dozing under the bamboo or fast asleep in the storage box, obviously recovering from his long trek. Amara that is, not the Amazon man. He very conveniently goes for a wander when we wish to reflect under the bamboo - which is appreciated - although he doesn't venture very far. Half-Sister thinks he is playing it safe due to having only one life left. I think he is just being a lazy cat. The Bookshelf informs me that cats sometimes sleep for up to sixteen hours a day. In the wild, this is to conserve energy for hunting. Who knows what they are conserving energy for in our street. The Wheezy Twins must be planning a safari trip, as they have clearly built up huge energy reserves over the years. In fact, sometimes you only know they are moving when a snail signals to overtake (judgemental thinking, back to homework). I should have known better than to suggest to The Bookshelf that The Wheezy Twins could be the slowest creatures in the world. No sooner had I said it than I realized my mistake. According to The Bookshelf, the three-toed sloth is the slowest animal in the world. They can only move at a maximum speed of 0.003 miles per hour, which means The Wheezy Twins would eventually pass them. Wandering Mind thinks this is a similar speed to Half-Sister when a trip to the vets is looming.

Last night, Half-Sister consulted The Bookshelf regarding what the Buddha actually said about the issue of worry and anxiety. She is gathering information to assist in the formulation of a plan aimed at tackling the debilitating anxiety that is currently stopping Amara from enjoying his final life on Earth. Interestingly enough, the Buddha said that worry and anxiety are a natural part of daily life. The thought that something unpleasant could happen in the future is our warning system - it is our mind giving us options, and telling us to be careful. However, sometimes things can get out of control so that everything appears a threat. This can lead us into avoidance mode. You only have to pay attention to Wandering Mind for a little while to understand that this is true. On a more positive note, it is always good to remember that most moments are not, in fact, anxious ones. Scientists, who are second in our eyes to The Bookshelf, believe that worry evolved in humans along with intelligence. Perhaps they worried about being too smart, or not smart enough.

In Buddhism, the fourth hindrance is restlessness and worry, or *uddhacca – kukkucca* in Pali. It is one of the Five Hindrances to Enlightenment, the other four being sensual desire, anger, sloth and torpor, and doubt. Boy, does The Bookshelf love that Pali translation book.

Half-Sister contemplates The Bookshelf's findings, paying special attention to the Buddha's words of wisdom. Eventually, she explains her thinking in a way only Half-Sister can - simple, but straight to the point. It appears to Half-Sister that Amara may be so anxious that he is avoiding everything in a futile attempt to conserve his last life. Of course, this is a forlorn and pointless quest; he is going to cop it sometime down the line as he is impermanent like the rest of us. Well, we think he is, The Bookshelf is still looking into that one. Trouble is, by avoiding everything and playing it safe, he is going to waste his final life. After a long period of reflection, Half-Sister decides that we will start integrating Amara back into the swing of things by teaching him to live in the present moment. She has decided that a good place to start the road to recovery is to encourage him to accompany us on our next walk around the river. After some Half-Sister persuasion, he eventually decides in favour of a quick lesson in walking meditation. Walking meditation is an excellent practice for taking your attention into the present moment. Getting your feet on the ground can allow you to move away from thinking mode and into the body - all useful if we are to get Amara shuffling his way around the river. However, not everyone is keen on this practice. Wandering Mind, for instance, resists joining in if she can help it as it supposedly makes her sleepy. We think her real issue is that it makes her slow down from her usual frantic pace. Of course, the issue in question is not solely confined to cats. Dad is a mindfulness teacher, and has worked with thousands of people suffering from anxiety. In fact, Half-Sister's plan for Amara is inspired by Dad's experience with a lady who was frightened to leave the house. All she wanted to do was to get on a bus and go into town for a coffee, and then travel home again. However, this simple task may as well have been to climb Mount Everest and then snowboard back down again. It was simply mission impossible in her mind. Dad's cunning plan was to condense this lady's journey down into small manageable pieces. He first of all asked her if one day she could walk to the garden gate at the front of her house, and then walk back again. It took a big effort, but she did it. After a while she plucked up the courage to walk to the bus stop. She didn't get on the bus, but again, the journey to and from was a major step. Eventually, she got on the bus and got off after one stop and walked home. Small steps, but progress. One day, she travelled into town and bought her coffee. She drank it, looking out the café window, a life transformed. For all I know she could be standing in the mountaineering shop at this very moment, her passport in one hand and a shiny new snowboard in the other. Every step she took was a meditation in itself. If you are reading this and thinking you would like to try a walking meditation, you can download a guided practice from our Dad's website (www.garyheads.co.uk). That plug should be worth a few treats.

Anyway, back to Amara and his tiny mindful steps. On the first day of Half-Sister's plan, Amara walks out of the storage box, and then walks back in again. This could take a while. One thing that is becoming apparent is that Amara's long trek to find Half-Sister has taken more out of him than we thought. For all we know, he may have lost some of those lives along the way. The Bookshelf, with his therapist's hat on, thinks Amara's unfaltering determination to find Half-Sister was the main factor in keeping his anxiety in check. Now that he has arrived, it has returned with a vengeance. Half-Sister will apply determination in equal measure, as it's the least our intrepid traveller deserves.

After a week, he makes it to the front garden, stands on the top step and peruses the vista. As he seems to show no visible signs of anxiety, his imposing presence in the street has the effect of turning every cat in the vicinity into a car mechanic, scurrying under the nearest vehicle. When we return from our walk around the river he is still there. Progress. Bit-by-bit he ventures a little farther until eventually he starts to follow us on our walks around the river. If anxiety gets the better of him he stops and tunes into his paws, grounding himself in the present moment.

Once Half-Sister is happy that Amara has cracked this part of her cunning plan, she begins to encourage him to be more mindful and widen his attention further.

He begins to take in the scenery, tune into physical sensations, and breathe in the aroma of the countryside. To our relief, he also starts venturing a little further away from Half-Sister. We are pleased to report that this has restored our reputation in the district. Having a moggy following your every move does nothing for your status as a fearless spaniel.

The spaniels who ate all the pies

It is on one such sojourn around the river that a strange incident occurs. Just as you approach the leafy path there is a small holding on the left-hand side. Over the years it has expanded, and now has horses, ducks, geese, sheep and a variety of out-buildings. Today it has something else. Just as we reach the field, the strange creatures prick up their ears and make a beeline for Half-Sister, Amara, and yours truly. By the time they reach the fence that surrounds the field, Amara had already taken a step back. Standing in front of our eyes are the fattest pair of spaniels you have ever seen. Well, we think they are spaniels. Wandering Mind has reservations, but the markings are similar, and their bums are wobbling fifty to the dozen. One thing is for certain - an apology is in order regarding the pies at the slimming club.

Wandering Mind has suggested that these two are giving spaniels a bad name and thinks we should endeavour to rectify the situation. We take a moment to put our heads together and formulate a course of action. They seem friendly enough, so they should be up for it. Half-Sister has remained silent so far, but as Wandering Mind and I have not had the steely look of disapproval, we crack on. Amara, on the other hand, is sitting on the fence - literally - and is currently shaking his head.

As no plan immediately springs to mind, we decide the best option is to head home and reflect under the bamboo. Half-Sister settles under the leafy canopy with the rest of us, but seems to have taken up the role of an impartial observer. Amara, meanwhile, remains disinterested in our mission, but has at least joined us under the bamboo for his afternoon snooze in the shade. Wandering Mind is in her element. She likes nothing better than

coming up with options (even though some are extreme to say the least). We do our best to describe the aforementioned spaniels to The Bookshelf, who listens to us carefully before deciding to place himself firmly in the dubious camp. Eventually, strange as it may seem, the best option appears to be to dress the spaniels in a headscarf and lipstick and enrol them in the slimming club. Nobody will know the difference, and it's not far for them to travel. We will put it to them tomorrow.

In the morning we awake to find Amara sitting under the bamboo next to the Buddha. After a quick wander around the back garden, we amble across and join him. Surprisingly, he greets us not with his customary nod, which we have become accustomed to, but by reciting a quote –

"You are a Buddha, and so is everyone else. I didn't make that up. It was the Buddha himself who said so. He said that all beings had the potential to become awakened. To practice walking meditation is to practice living in mindfulness. Mindfulness and enlightenment are one. Enlightenment leads to mindfulness and mindfulness leads to enlightenment."

Half-Sister loves the quote and enquires as to where it originates from. She is also curious as to how Amara discovered it in the first place. He informs us that The Bookshelf shared it and that it is by Thich Nhat Hanh. He follows this up by explaining that Thich Nhat Hanh comes from Vietnam in South East Asia, the same place those pot-bellied pigs in the field come from.

Later that evening, after the safe return of Mum's headscarf and lipstick, we settle in the dining room with The Bookshelf. He is finding it difficult to hold a serious conversation with us due to the pot-bellied pig situation. Our explanation of it being a simple misunderstanding that anyone could make is carrying very little weight in this house. Wandering Mind has been unusually quiet today. Half-Sister, although amused, has more serious matters on her mind. After her cheesy grin subsides, she gets around to asking The Bookshelf about Amara's quote. She thinks it was very appropriate, and thanks The Bookshelf for sharing it with him. He informs us that he is always happy to share quotes, however that was not the quote he shared with Amara. That cat is full of surprises.

The next day, Half-Sister continues her work with Amara regarding his anxiety and the belief he holds that he only has one life left. She falls back on her tried and tested teaching, gleaned from the Buddha, that we should question everything until we truly believe it for ourselves. With this in mind, she challenges Amara over his belief that cats actually have nine lives to start with. Half-Sister is not going in blind here. The Bookshelf has checked it all out and reckons there is no hard and fast evidence, scientific or otherwise, to prove the theory is true. Amara is far from convinced, but Half-Sister keeps at it. She suggests that cats might just be adventurous, and proposes that their natural agility gets them out of dangerous situations, but not always. His reply is that the myth has been past down for centuries, and nobody has questioned it before. Half-Sister is prepared for that one, and turns her attention to The Bookshelf, who has been listening to the conversation with great interest. She asks him to define the word myth.

'A myth is an age old story that was never based on fact'.

Amara has a deep frown on his forehead and looks thoughtful. This is skilful stuff from Half-Sister however, the best is yet to come. She slowly and deliberately raises her paw, and once again moves into story-telling mode. Splendid. Half-Sister encourages Amara to pay attention as she prepares to tell him an ancient Japanese story. He duly obliges, and closes his eyes to aid the process.

A great Zen Buddhist master, who was in charge of the Mayu Kagi monastery, had a cat which was his true passion in life. So, during meditation classes, he kept the cat by his side in order to make the most of his company. One morning, the master, who was already quite old, passed away. His best disciple took his place. "What shall we do with the cat?" asked the other monks. As a tribute to the memory of their old instructor, the new master decided to allow the cat to continue attending the Zen Buddhist classes.

Some disciples from the neighbouring monasteries travelling through those parts discovered that in one of the region's most renowned temples, a cat took part in the meditation sessions. The story began to spread. Many years passed. The cat died, but as the students at the monastery were so used to its presence, they soon found another cat. Meanwhile, the other temples began introducing cats into their meditation sessions: they believed the cat was truly responsible for the fame and excellence of Mayu Kagi's teaching.

A generation passed, and technical treatises began to appear about the importance of the cat in Zen meditation. A university professor developed a thesis, which was accepted by the academic community, that felines have the ability to increase human concentration and eliminate negative energy. And so, for a whole century, the cat was considered an essential part of Zen Buddhist studies in that region.

Until a master appeared who was allergic to animal hair, and decided to remove the cat from his daily exercises with the students. There was a fierce negative reaction, but the master insisted. Since he was an excellent instructor, the students continued to make the same progress, in spite of the absence of the cat.

Little by little, the monasteries, always in search of new ideas and already tired of having to feed so many cats, began eliminating the animals from the classes. In twenty years, new revolutionary theories began to appear with very convincing titles such as 'The Importance of Meditating Without a Cat', or 'Balancing the Zen Universe by Will Power Alone, Without the Help of Animals.'

Another century passed, and the cat withdrew completely from the meditation rituals in that region. But two hundred years were necessary for everything to return to normal, because during all this time, no one asked why the cat was there.

Half-Sister leaves it at that, and heads to the kitchen for a well-earned drink. Hours later, Amara can be seen sitting under the bamboo in the back garden, contemplating. He has been there a long time. He has his head resting on the Buddha's lap, and his eyes are closed tight. The Bookshelf is most impressed with Half-Sister's argument and agrees entirely with her thesis. He especially likes her use of the cat story and wonders where she got that from, as it is certainly not in his library. Half-Sister explains that it is taken from the book 'Like a Flowing River' by Paul Coelho. Before The Bookshelf can ask the inevitable question, Half-Sister tells him it was Mum who found the story, she keeps the book in her bedroom. There are no more books to be borrowed, as the library is closed for the night.

Reflections under the bamboo

Half-Sister seems to be making good progress with Amara - he looks more relaxed these days and is venturing further away from the house to explore the terrain. He can often be seen wandering in the woods at the back of the garden, a far cry from when he first arrived. There are, however, one or two things that don't quite add up. For starters, there is the meaning of his name. It is a complete contradiction to his fear, anxiety and last-life theory. Half-Sister and The Bookshelf have been pondering this one, and are intrigued. Even more interesting is who actually gave him the name in the first place? Then there is the quote that appeared out of nowhere and was contrary to The Bookshelf's take on things. Finally, how did he know the fat spaniels were, indeed, Vietnamese pot-bellied pigs? There are more holes in his story than our bedtime quilt, and that's a lot of holes. The plot thickens.

P. S.

The Bookshelf is back to normal after emerging from his self-imposed huff. He has forgiven Half-Sister and Mum, and has ordered the book from Amazon. Tickety-boo re-alignment has been achieved.

5

The Phenomena called Jessica

"I visualize a time when we will be to robots what dogs are to humans.
And I am rooting for the machines."

Claude Shannon

Wandering Mind reckons that when Jessica has accumulated enough information,
she will energize herself back to the mothership.

WE ARE AWOKEN FROM our slumber today by the sound of footsteps bounding up the steps to the front door. There is no barking or spinning in circles as the doorbell rings twice. The only action taken is by The Bookshelf, who puts his book down in anticipation. Amara is still in his garden storage box pretending to be a lawnmower, so is totally unaware of today's development. The reason for this lack of activity is not laziness or disinterest; it's familiarity. We know those footsteps well - it's the Amazon man. Unusually, there is an eagerness in Mum's footsteps as she puts down her tea towel and heads for the front door. She is far too enthusiastic for it to be our dog food; however, The Bookshelf's wish for a new addition to his collection is still a distinct possibility. Pleasantries exchanged, Mum returns to the kitchen with a small box in her hand, The Bookshelf sighs with disappointment. We are now up on our paws, and not adverse to the odd spin. We are curious - perhaps you can eat it, after all. Now Dad is bounding down the stairs from his office to inspect the box. There is not much that gets him out of his work space, so this must be exciting. He encourages Mum to open it. Once all the packaging has been dispensed with, a black cylindrical-shaped thingy emerges like some robot creature from outer space. Where's Captain Kirk when you need him? Mum plugs it into the wall and, much to our amazement, it produces a purple spin. Now there have been some shenanigans going on in the world of dogs lately, what with cockapoos, labradoodles, sprockers, and sprollies. to name but a few, but surely not a springerbot? Much to our relief, Half-Sister has spotted the words 'Virtual Assistant' on the side of the box. If a purple spin wasn't enough to contend with, Dad then proceeds to ask it a question. He ponders for a while before asking our new alien buddy who the Buddha was. The purple spin returns, followed by a detailed analysis of the life of the Buddha - all this delivered in a sultry robotic female voice. The last few words of her explanation are drowned out by the sound of books falling onto the dining room floor. After a thorough inspection and test by Mum and Dad, the new addition to the household is deemed fit for purpose and is carefully positioned next to the lamp in the living room. Half-Sister declares that it is unkind to continue calling her our alien buddy, therefore, as we have ascertained the said virtual assistant is female, we decide to christen her Jessica. We ask our virtual assistant if she is happy to be called Jessica; she informs us that she doesn't have an opinion about it, so we take that as a yes. So far today, Jessica has performed admirably. In fact, she has not failed to answer one question she has been asked. She has told Mum what the weather is going to be like today; played Radio Four and told a variety of jokes (most of them bad). Half-Sister is watching from afar, and weighing this little girl up. According to the instruction manual she learns all the time, listens to everything and can even order stuff on Amazon. Now that's handy. Wandering Mind reckons that when Jessica has accumulated enough information, she will energize herself back to the mothership. Jessica replies with a purple spin, and then proceeds to play the theme tune from the film 'Close Encounters'. Our new acquaintance has a wicked sense of humour, much to the annoyance of Wandering Mind.

Later in the day, we all head out for a walk with Dad. Amara, who has finally vacated the storage box, continues his rehabilitation by following several yards behind. As we pass the field next to the small holding, we do our best to not look embarrassed. If we could whistle, we would - as we can't, we make do with looking down at the ground as if we have found something interesting. The pot-bellied pigs are happily frolicking in the mud and munching on cabbages. It is difficult for Wandering Mind not to imagine them in a headscarf and lipstick, but she is doing her best. Half-way round the river we suddenly realise that as Mum has gone to the shops and we are all out on our walk, The Bookshelf and Jessica have been left alone in the house. The Bookshelf has not said a word since Jessica arrived, whereas she has not stopped talking. Half-Sister thinks it might be helpful that they spend a little time together. After all, The Bookshelf has always been our fountain of knowledge. Who knows how he feels now that there is a new kid on the block? Time will tell whether The Bookshelf sees Jessica as a threat or as his trusty assistant. When we get back to the house, we soon realise that none of the above possibilities were indeed accurate. The Bookshelf has rearranged his books in alphabetical order while we have been away, and seems to have an extra shine to his wood. Meanwhile, Jessica has added a red glow to her purple spin, which seems to be rotating a tad faster than normal. As we enter the dining room, we are just in time to see The Bookshelf slide a book of poetry back to its rightful place. Interesting. As The Bookshelf is positioned against the dining room wall, we wonder if there is a side to him we have not seen before.

It's raining cats and dogs

The following day, Mum skips down the stairs and asks Jessica for today's weather forecast. She duly obliges: torrential rain, gale force winds, thunder and lightning. She then proceeds to add an amber weather warning for effect. Half-Sister suggests that due to the adverse weather conditions, our time in the garden will be limited. She therefore declares today a study day. The Bookshelf is delighted, and immediately prepares his numerous books on the Buddha's teachings. Jessica throws out a purple spin with a hint of red. As we start to assemble in the dining room, we can see through the window that the rain is already heavy, and that the bamboo is bending and swaying in the wind. Everyone is heading for cover, including The Ginger One Next Door, who is slinking home like a ginger biscuit that has been dunked in a cup of tea for too long. His partner in crime, The Siamese, is not far behind him. He decides to stay at The Ginger One's house rather than travel the extra few yards to his own house. Typical. Our Dad is working from home today, and is currently ensconced in his office. Mum, as usual, is in her sewing room making another quilt. This one has colourful houses on it. Let's hope it doesn't end up in a state. They are currently engaged in a conversation, albeit through the adjoining wall. The subject of this dialogue is Amara. It seems they are concerned about his welfare due to the inclement weather, and are considering bringing him into the house for the night. This will be the first time a cat has walked through the door of this house since Tabitha and Cleo, the cats who lived here before us. By all accounts, Tabitha was laid back, wise and a bit feisty. Cleo was the mega-friendly one, and a bit bonkers. Mum thinks it's strange how we seem to have inherited some of their traits. What a cheek! Fancy calling Half-Sister bonkers. After the initial shock of this revelation subsides slightly, Half-Sister reminds us that compassion for all beings is at the heart of the Buddha's teachings. With that statement reverberating in our dangly ears, she heads for the back door to invite Amara to the study day. A few minutes later, two water-logged beings return to the dining room with accompanying puddles. Mum, having popped downstairs to make a cup of tea, follows the small river from the kitchen to the dining room. Upon seeing the squelchy versions of Half-Sister and Amara, she relays a message to Dad that the problem of Amara has been solved. For one foolish moment, Mum considers trying to dry Half-Sister with a towel; it is only a fleeting thought, as she knows only too well that this is one of Half-Sister's favourite games.

In honour of Amara's presence and our new virtual assistant Jessica, who we know will be listening, today's study day is entitled *The Dharma: The Teachings of the*

Buddha. Half-Sister starts the study day as always with a short guided meditation. Dignified postures all round (although Amara seems to sit in a dignified posture continuously). She aptly chooses a sound meditation as there is certainly plenty to be mindful of outside. We think Jessica may have underestimated the weather forecast, as it is currently monsoon-like in the back garden. Wandering Mind has joined us, and has resurrected her bright-yellow anorak especially for the occasion. We have not seen this outfit since last year's mountain meditation. She appears to be in a disruptive mood today; this is probably due to Amara being in the house, and the extra-terrestrial one yet to return to the mothership. Eventually she settles down and turns her attention to the sound meditation. When the practice is over, we open our eyes and settle in for Half-Sister's talk. She has a bigger audience than normal today. The Buddha's teachings, or sermons as they were sometimes called, pointed towards the true nature of the Universe. In Buddhism, this is known as The Dharma. He gave his first sermon on the outskirts of a city called Varanasi, in a deer park called Sarnath. Varanasi is also known as Benares, and is situated on the banks of the River Ganga in Utter Pradesh, India. This first sermon was called *The Setting in Motion of the Wheel of Dharma Sutta.* The Bookshelf apologises to Half-Sister for interrupting, and tells us that in Pali it is *The Dhammaacakkappavattana Sutta.* Wow! Did The Bookshelf just use every letter in the alphabet there? Half-Sister continues. The sermon sets out an overview of suffering and a way out of suffering. This is referred to as *The Four Noble Truths*. You could perhaps describe the Buddha as a physician; he first diagnoses the illness, and then suggests a medicine to cure it. Half-Sister then explains, in simple language, the Buddha's plan to end suffering. Amara, meanwhile, remains in his dignified posture. He looks as if he is listening intently, or asleep. It's hard to tell. As he has positioned himself next to the radiator, steam is gently rising from his body. It looks as if he is overthinking, and his thoughts are evaporating into thin air. The so called *"illness"* that the Buddha diagnosed in human beings is called dukkha (suffering). He spoke of there being three types of dukkha. The first is mental and physical pain. Then there is the suffering that arises from change - everything is impermanent. Finally, there is the suffering that is created by the failure to recognise that no *"I"* stands alone. Everything and everyone is conditioned and interdependent. The Buddha followed all this up by telling us that suffering is caused by desire and grasping. So to crave, desire or grasp for something we don't have is a principal cause of suffering. As mentioned before, everything is impermanent and constantly changing, so trying to hold on to something is a futile act. It is doomed to fail. It's like trying to stop a spaniel's bum from wobbling by giving it a treat. The good news is that it is possible to put an end to all this suffering, and to gain freedom from the constant sense of uneasiness. The way out is through *The Noble Eightfold Path*. "What is *The Noble Eightfold Path?*" you may ask. Half-Sister is about to tell us. To move along the path that leads to freedom from suffering, we have to practise and develop habits of ethical conduct, thought and meditation. Amara opens one eye and shuffles slightly away from the radiator. He then asks Half-Sister to explain just what these practices are. I have noticed that he seems to have a habit of opening his dodgy eye and saving his good one for later. Half-Sister lists the practices of *The Noble Eightfold Path,* and then proceeds to explain each one. In the background we can hear the shuffling of pages. There is no way on this earth that The Bookshelf will not give us the Pali translation for each one.

The Noble Eightfold Path

Right Understanding (*Samma ditthi*)
Right Thought (*Samma sankappa*)
Right Speech (*Samma vaca*)
Right Action (*Samma kammanta*)
Right Livelihood (*Samma ajiva*)
Right Effort (*Samma vayama*)
Right Mindfulness (*Samma sati*)
Right Concentration (*Samma samadhi*)

Amara closes his dodgy eye and settles in once again, as Half-Sister begins to explain each practice. Just before she begins there is a whisper from the living room in a sultry robotic voice. "I knew all that." Resisting the temptation to put Jessica on the spot by asking her to explain each practice, Half-Sister instead cracks on. The

Bookshelf seems disappointed for reasons only known to himself.

The eight practices, or factors, are aimed at promoting ethical conduct (*sila*), mental discipline (*samadhi*) and wisdom (*panna*). Returning for a moment to the wooden one known as The Bookshelf, it seems to us that he has developed some kind of Pali Tourette Syndrome. No sooner does Half-Sister mention a word from the Buddha's teachings than the Pali translation arrives at a speed of knots. Half-Sister must have the patience of a saint, as she never barks a word at the constant interruptions. On reflection, I think The Bookshelf is either showing off or feels under pressure. It is no coincidence that this behaviour all began with the arrival of the purple spinning cylindrical one. Before Half-Sister continues further, Wandering Mind vacates the dining room, and so ends her participation in the study day. Apparently The Bookshelf is doing her head in. Her words, not mine.

Ethical Conduct
Ethical conduct (*sila*) is built on universal love and compassion for all living beings. There are two qualities that should be developed equally: compassion (*karuna*) and wisdom (*panna*). In this section there are three factors of the path: right speech, right action and right livelihood. Amara nods his head either in understanding or approval. There is no sound from the living room; Jessica is either keeping quiet or is busy adding it to her ever-growing database of information.

Right Speech

Right Speech means not telling any porkies for starters. No backbiting, slander, harsh, rude or abusive language. It also includes no idle, useless, foolish babble and gossip. Wandering Mind would have very little to say if she followed that last bit. So in a nutshell, speak the truth and speak in a friendly, gentle, meaningful and useful manner. Be careful with your words, and if you can't say anything useful, keep quiet. A further whisper follows from the living room as Jessica proclaims she is verbally enlightened.

Right Action

Right action promotes moral, honourable and peaceful conduct. We should not destroy life, steal or indulge in sexual misconduct. The least said about Half-Sister and I having the same mum but two different dads the better. Finally, we should endeavour to help others whenever we can.

Right Livelihood

This means making one's living by a profession that does not bring harm to others. This would include trading in weapons, alcohol, killing animals etc.

These three factors of *The Noble Eightfold Path* constitute ethical conduct. It is the general consensus that no spiritual development is possible without this moral basis.

Mental Discipline

The Bookshelf seems to have got the Pali Tourettes under

control for the time being, which is perfect timing, as Wandering Mind has returned for this section of the study day. She suggests that the mental discipline section is the equivalent of her being drawn at home in the cup – a clear advantage and every chance of winning. The three factors in mental discipline are right effort, right mindfulness and right concentration.

Right Effort

Right effort is cultivating the energy and will to prevent unwholesome states of mind from arising. To eliminate unwholesome states of mind that have arisen, and produce wholesome states of mind. Tricky stuff when Wandering Mind goes off on one. Which is often.

Right Mindfulness

Right mindfulness is to become aware, mindful and attentive with regard to the body (sensations/feelings) and the mind (thoughts, ideas etc). The skill of mindfulness is developed by practising meditation. By paying attention, we can learn to be with pleasant, unpleasant and neutral sensations in the body, and thoughts in the mind. Concentrating on the breath is one of the well-known practices used to pay attention to body and mind (*anapanasati*).

Right Concentration

Developing the ability to bring the dispersed and distracted mind to a centre, to see clearly. Thus the mind is trained, disciplined and developed through right effort, right mindfulness and right concentration. Wandering Mind folds her arms and looks around the room defiantly.

Wisdom

The final two factors, right thought and right understanding, constitute wisdom in *The Noble Eightfold Path*.

Right Thought

Right thought denotes thoughts of renunciation or detachment, thoughts of love and non-violence towards all living beings.

Right Understanding

Right understanding is the understanding of things as they are. This is the highest wisdom which sees the Ultimate Reality. Real, deep understanding is seeing things in its true nature, without name and label. This is only possible when the mind is free from impurities developed through the practice of meditation.

So ends Half-Sister's brief account of *The Noble Eightfold Path*. She sums up by telling us that it is a way of life to be followed and practised. It is self-discipline in body, word and mind. We are to remember that it is not about belief, prayer, worship or ceremony. It is also not religious - it is a path leading to the realization of the Ultimate Truth and freedom.

Half-Sister then takes a rest after her exertions. The Bookshelf is most impressed by her skilful explanation, and files away his teachings of the Buddha collection.

They were not needed today. Amara opens both his eyes and nods at Half-Sister. Meanwhile, in the living room a tiny whisper emerges from within a purple spin. "Blimey, I didn't know all that, but I do now."

As evening arrives it is still raining and blowing a gale outside (whoever she is). Large puddles are forming in the back garden, and the Buddha seems to be residing on his own private island. We are all stretched out on the sofa, whilst Mum and Dad are reading. It's a scene of domestic bliss. Meanwhile, in the dining room Amara is curled up under the radiator. We think it will have been a long time since he was that cosy. Dad's book is about Buddhism, which is not surprising. It's a new one, and The Bookshelf is impatient for him to finish it so he can read it. Suddenly, Dad turns to Jessica and asks her a question about the Buddha. There is a pause, followed by the customary purple spin. She then, to the amazement of all present, recites Half-Sister's talk word for word. Wandering Mind returns, still adorned in her yellow anorak, and suggests that this is further proof that she is indeed an alien. Although a Russian spy, and worst still, the Inland Revenue, have entered her head.

Reflections under the bamboo

We are pleased to report that the rain has finally stopped. This was confirmed by Wandering Mind, who eventually removed her yellow anorak to celebrate the occasion. Amara has returned to the garden storage box, but now wanders in and out of the house unannounced. Nobody seems to mind. His favourite spot is under the radiator next to The Bookshelf. They seem to get on well. The Bookshelf took a shine to him after Amara enquired if he had any books by the Dalai Lama. Whenever Amara sees Half-Sister, he asks her more questions about the Buddha, and The Noble Eightfold Path. As the saying goes, 'curiosity killed the cat,' so he needs to be careful with that last life of his. Sometimes it's as if he is testing her knowledge of the subject. Meanwhile, Jessica continues to listen and learn. If only she knew some better jokes.

What do you call a wolf who picks up litter after campers and is worried about pollution?

Aware wolf

6

The Moggy Meditation Group are Revolting

"At night, when the sky is full of stars, and the sea is still, you get the wonderful sensation that you are floating in space."

Natalie Wood

For the first time ever, Half-Sister has called an emergency board meeting.

AMARA'S ARRIVAL, AND HIS subsequent sleepover, seems to have been accepted by most. The Bookshelf has warmed to him, as has the radiator, and Half-Sister is now on a mission to sort out his anxiety once and for all. Personally, I think he is a bit shifty, but will give him the benefit of the doubt. For now. Wandering Mind is yet to have an opinion on the matter as all her time is currently being spent on Jessica-watch. As Jessica has no data on Amara, she has decided in her wisdom to hold noble silence. Taking into consideration her recent form, this is unusual to say the least. It appears that Mum and Dad don't mind having an adopted cat floating about the place, so all appears to be in line with the Buddha's teachings of love and compassion. Or so we thought.

For the first time ever, Half-Sister has called an emergency board meeting. The Bookshelf is excited at the prospect, as he loves structure and debate. I didn't know we even had a board to meet - it turns out we have. Members present include Half-Sister, The Bookshelf, yours truly and Wandering Mind, who has volunteered to take notes. Amara is also present, due to the fact that he is entwined with the radiator. Jessica is listening as usual and, without being asked, spins out the definition of a board meeting.

A formal meeting of the board of directors of an organisation, held usually at definite intervals to consider policy issues and major problems. Presided over by a chairperson of the organisation, it must meet the quorum requirements and the deliberations must be recorded in the minutes.

As we have not had a board meeting before, let alone

an emergency one, the virtual assistant's definition is most helpful. Taking everything into consideration, it looks as if we are about to deliberate a major problem. Sure enough there is an issue, and Half-Sister wants everyone's input to help resolve it. The focus of our attention and the reason we have been summoned is down to the behaviour of the motley crew known as the moggy meditation group. Half-Sister gathers her thoughts and then proceeds to give us an overview of the issue in question. As her analysis has been gathered using spaniel intuition, there is absolutely no point whatsoever in doubting her findings. After a year of dedicated practice and study, the moggy meditation group have suddenly lost the plot and are revolting. The first sign of trouble was signalled by The Ginger One Next Door who turned up late for a session. This is unheard of, as he is always out to impress Half-Sister. Not only that, but his dignified posture was more like that of a huffy child that had just been told off for bad timekeeping. His sidekick, The Siamese slinked in even later, his tail swishing faster than Dad's windscreen wipers on maximum. Initially The White One appeared to be the blackleg of the group by defying the moggy union and arriving on time. However, after perusing his black-tipped tail as normal, he then turned his back on Half-Sister. It is probably just as well he didn't break ranks, as calling him a blackleg to go with his black-tipped tail may have pushed him over the edge. To top it all off The Ginger One then produced a vets note on behalf of The Wheezy Twins. In Half-Sister's opinion, this sulky defiance has been going on for long enough. Hence the emergency board meeting.

We all listen intently as Half-Sister carefully explains her intuition-based theory. Following a year of uninterrupted attention, she thinks the moggy meditation group have found the arrival of Amara challenging. Not only that, he is allowed to stay in her back garden, and on occasions even reside in the house close to their spiritual leader. In other words, they are racked with jealousy and envy, and are currently residing in the Land of Strop. Half-Sister explains that a period of loving-kindness meditation practice would probably be the prescribed antidote by the Buddha. However, as they are either currently unwilling to engage or AWOL, something more creative may be required. To help us understand what might be going on in the heads of the aforementioned moggies, Half-Sister once again refers to the teachings of the Buddha. If her theory is correct, it is the powerful effect of jealousy and envy that is causing the catastrophic uprising. According to the Buddha, jealousy and envy are similar in that they are both negative emotions. They also have the ability to destroy relationships, something Half-Sister is keen to avoid. Envy is strongly linked to greed and desire, whilst both emotions have connections to anger. Jealousy is defined as a resentment towards others who possess something we think should belong to us. It is often accompanied by possessiveness, a sense of insecurity, and betrayal. As the Buddha clarified in his teachings, the root of these emotions is the belief of a permanent self. The Bookshelf has stated on many occasions that this belief is an illusion. Half-Sister pulls all the threads of thought together like a fisherman gathering his catch: the moggy meditation group is jealous because they think someone has taken something that belongs to them. They are envious because they think someone is more fortunate than they are. In reality, it is all an illusion; however, someone needs to explain that to them, and it won't be me. Amara, who has been silent throughout Half-Sister's explanation, suddenly pipes up that in his opinion, what is required here is motivation. He thinks that if Half-Sister's theory is correct, and he has a feeling she is right, then the current situation has de-motivated the group. As it appears to be his arrival that has caused the moggies to revolt, he feels a certain responsibility to restore peace and tranquillity. Amara appears to have taken a leaf out of Half-Sister's book and has prepared a cunning plan that will bring them back into the fold. He politely asks Half-Sister if she will agree to him putting the plan into action. If he is successful, she can then introduce the loving-kindness meditations and all should be well. The board passes the resolution, although we forgot to ask what his plan is. I guess we will find out soon enough.

The following day, Amara sets up an office under the bamboo and proceeds to summon each member of the moggy meditation group for a personal interview. They were never going to say no to him, however, how he contacted them remains a mystery. He conveniently forgets to mention the behaviour issue, and instead informs them that Half-Sister has given him permission to teach the group a new meditation. This is half true - we did agree on the plan, but there was no mention of a meditation. Perhaps he was a politician in a past life. Amara suggests that because the meditation is a secret and ancient practice, it might be better if they meet up in the woods at the back of the garden. The moggy meditation group agree, and leave with a purposeful stride and a twinkle in their eye. He can spin a yarn, can Amara.

In the afternoon, the moggy meditation group congregate in the woods as previously arranged. Amara is already waiting for them. They shuffle themselves into a circle and immediately take up a dignified posture without being asked. Half-Sister has trained them well. The Bookshelf told me that a group of cats is sometimes called a clowder or a glaring. I'm not sure The Siamese would be allowed in the glaring group - those peepers would cause mayhem. When I asked The Bookshelf what the definition of a group of spaniels was, he looked me straight in the eye and replied, "trouble". As he said it with a wooden expression, I have filed the comment in the sarcasm file. Anyway, back to the job in hand. I have been despatched into the garden by Half-Sister under the pretence that I am practising my tennis ball aerobics. In actual fact I am an undercover agent, which is apparently a step up from a decoy (my previous occupation). With one eye on the ball and one ear listening to the secret meeting in the woods, my career as a spy begins. Amara starts the gathering of huffy mousers by explaining that through the practice of meditation it is actually possible to acquire the skill of levitation, and to even fly. The moggy meditation group look to the heavens as a collection of assorted birds fly worriedly overhead. He tells them that Tibetan masters can levitate and fly, and then backs up the statement with an eye-witness account. The first Westerner to observe the phenomenon was Marco Polo. He encountered a Tibetan Lama who levitated over seven hundred years ago. I am not sure if this discovery was pre or post his famous mint period, or if he had even opened any of his Italian restaurants by then. I suppose in the context of levitation and flying, that thought is irrelevant, but interesting all the same. Amara continues. Traditional Tibetan literature also records details of Buddhist mystics who had acquired the skill of flight. The Buddha was also said to be partial to a bit of levitation and flying, and had apparently done so on several occasions. Amara knows his stuff; he has the moggies eating out of his hand, and you can see they are eager to get cracking. With the pre-amble over, he gets down to some serious medita-tion. The group seems to have spread out slightly. Perhaps they are anticipating instant results and are clearing the runway. As they have their eyes closed, I decide to inch forward a little to acquire a better view. If any of these moggies get off the ground, I don't want to miss the spectacle, especially The Wheezy twins. If they take off it will be like watching a giant helicopter slowly lifting into the blue yonder. It will go viral on the Internet in an instant. Unfortunately, my skill as an undercover agent has yet to be mastered, as The Siamese has spotted me and sent one of his peepers my way. Time to skedaddle back to Half-Sister and de-brief.

I carefully explain what was said, and practised, in the confines of the woods. Unfortunately, due to a siamezy intervention, the end result remains a mystery. The Bookshelf confirms that Amara is indeed being factual in his description of levitation, and with his statements regarding Tibetan lamas and mystics. Much to Half-Sister's delight, the Buddha did apparently levitate on occasions. We don't know if it was on special occasions or just when he felt like it. Half-Sister is curious to uncover what else Amara gleaned from his time at the Tibetan monastery; so far he has been full of surprises. After what seems like an age, Amara finally waltzes into the dining room and slides his black body back under the welcoming heat of the radiator. As the engineer has been to service the central heating today, the radiator is in fine form. It seems Amara has acquired many additional followers from his trip into the woods. In addition to his new levitation disciples, he has also returned with an army of spiky burrs. We know all about them - they are determined little characters. Mum has spent many an evening picking them out of our ears after a woodland walk. Just before Amara closes his eyes for a well-earned nap, he tells Half-Sister that it's 'job done' and it's over to her. We can only surmise that no cats have mastered the skill of levitation just yet; this will be a relief to the bird population and the local squirrels. Jessica flashes a purple spin, and suggests that if one of cats actually makes it off the ground it will be all over Twitter. We think that was a joke, but are not sure.

On the next moggy meditation practice day, Half-Sister arrives early. She sits in her dignified posture under the bamboo in anticipation of a full house - she is not disappointed. They are all present and correct and awaiting instructions. Even The White One is facing the right way today, and The Wheezy Twins have arrived safely minus a vets note, although one of them seems to have a acquired a limp. Let's hope it's due to a touch of arthritis rather than a crash landing from levitation practice. Half-Sister proceeds to guide the session in her usual fashion. The meditation is loving-kindness, and the dharma talk is all about compassion and empathy for others. Everything looks to have returned to factory settings, if that is applicable to cats. Amara has been true to his word. Before the session ends, Half-Sister decides to give the group the heads-up about unrealistic expectations. She broaches the subject of levitation, and tells the group not to be disappointed if they fail to master the skill. After all, it's an ancient practice and could take a long time to bear fruit. If they practise their meditation every day and attend the weekly practice sessions, who knows what can be achieved. They seem to be happy with that, and promise Half-Sister that they will practise diligently in the future. The Ginger One Next Door adds that Amara told them that it was simply mind over matter. The Siamese nods his head in agreement, and informs Half-Sister that no further encouragement is required, as the sight of Amara levitating was motivation enough.

Reflections under the bamboo

Since Amara's timely intervention and Half-Sister's dharma talk on loving-kindness and compassion, the moggy meditation group appear to have eased back into normality. There has been no further need for emergency board meetings. The Ginger One Next Door and The Siamese have acquired a steely determination when it comes to their meditation practice; they seem set on cracking the levitation code and flying off to pastures anew. We are currently keeping an eye on how they make their way to the top of parked cars in the street to assess any progress they may be making. It's their favourite place to hang-out, and although it is unlikely they will master the skill any time soon, funnier things have happened. As for Amara, he continues to come to terms with his anxiety, and is fast becoming a fixture in the house. If he spends any more time under the radiator, Dad will add him to the central heating service contract. Half-Sister and The Bookshelf continue to unravel the conundrum that Amara is, and have a growing list of strange occurrences and unusual skills to investigate. I am continuing to hone my tennis ball skills in the back garden. I think it would be wise to up my game in case a levitating tom cat flies by.

7

My Monastery is bigger than your Monastery

*"What counts is not necessarily the size of the dog in the fight -
it's the size of the fight in the dog."*

Dwight D. Eisenhower

*Half-Sister has instructed us that she is going to instigate a conversation with
Amara about the time Dad took us to the Buddhist monastery.*

AFTER ALL HALF-SISTER'S HARD work, Amara finally appears to be getting to grips with his anxiety and uneasiness. He has made himself at home in the garden storage box and frequents the dining room when it's raining. I have noticed that he can often be found under the radiator next to The Bookshelf, even if there is only a slight chance of rain or simply the potential of a grey cloud to arrive. Last night, Half-Sister, The Bookshelf and yours truly discussed the enigma called Amara. Since his arrival, one or two things have emerged that definitely need further investigation. Now that he seems more settled, Half-Sister thinks a gentle interrogation is in order. He has told us about his time in a monastery in Tibet, but little else - even that was a little sketchy, to say the least. We know that a monk taught him to meditate, and presumably to also levitate, but we wonder - what other 'tates' has he in the locker? We await a rainy day, or a wandering cloud.

One of the advantages of living in the North East of England is that you do not have to wait long for rain clouds to appear. As if we had ordered it on Amazon, the heavens open and Amara is ensconced under the radiator. Perfect. Half-Sister has instructed us that she is going to instigate a conversation with Amara about the time Dad took us to the Buddhist monastery. Wandering Mind still has the notes she carefully collected on that fateful day, although they may not be needed, as the visit is engraved in Half-Sister's memory. She asks Amara if he would like to hear about her visit, and suggests that it will pass the time until the storm subsides. He nods and opens both eyes. This is followed by a stretch, before he drops into his now customary dignified posture. Half-Sister starts the story from the time she entered the Dharma Hall, just prior to the beginning of Evening Puja. She comments on the absence of the Lhasa Apso dog. He is supposedly the guardian of Buddhist monasteries, but apparently not on the day we visited. Amara remarks that he met a few Lhasa Apsos when he was in Tibet. He says they were friendly enough, but seemed to be happy wanderers. That figures. Before The Bookshelf can add to the Lhasa Apso biography, a purple spin materialises through the storm-induced darkness.

"The Lhasa Apso is a smallish breed that originates in Tibet. It was bred as a guard dog for Buddhist monasteries to alert the Monks of intruders. 'Lhasa' is the capital of Tibet and 'Apso' translated into English means 'bearded'. The timeline for the breed is unknown, but they have been around for thousands of years. They were domesticated and actively bred as long ago as 800 BC, making them one of the oldest recognised breeds" The Bookshelf is going to have to up his game here.

Half-Sister shuffles her paws and begins to set the scene. She describes in great detail the Theravadin monks in their splendid saffron-coloured robes, their shaved heads and impeccable dignified postures. She lingers over the description of the huge Buddha towering over the Dharma Hall and its participants, even pointing out the colour and shape of the flowers that reside either side of the Buddha's statue. Before Half-Sister continues further, she casts a line into the pool of inquisition by asking Amara if his monastery in Tibet was similar to hers. For

a while it looks as if the question has fallen on deaf ears,
until eventually he tells us that his monastery was more
like a palace than a monastery. We all lean forward in
anticipation of further revelations. The silence seems
endless. I thought about mentioning the old pulling teeth
metaphor, but after Half-Sister's recent adventure
thought better of it. Eventually, Amara adds that the
monks wore maroon robes. That's it. The silence
returns, like a long lost boomerang - you are pleased to
see it until it smacks you in the mush. Half-Sister is about
to resume when The Bookshelf decides to intervene. In
his usual imperturbable manner, he states that saffron
robes are worn by monks practising Theravadin Buddhism, whilst maroon robes are worn by monks in the
Mahayana tradition (Tibetan Buddhism). Amara nods in
agreement. It appears that the purple spinning one didn't
know that. Of course, she does now. The Bookshelf,
being the wise soul that he is, decides to join Half-Sister
on her fishing expedition. He casts his net into the sea
and trawls the depths of subterfuge. Wandering Mind
suggests that was my best metaphor to date. It's nice to
be appreciated, although I think I may be in danger of
contracting the same ailment that struck down The
Bookshelf and his Pali translations. Anyway, back to
fishing. The Bookshelf reveals to Amara that he doesn't
know the difference between Theravada and Mahayana
Buddhism. Luckily for us, neither does Jessica. Either
that or she has donned a purple anorak and spun out her
line. Everyone is looking at Amara, who has so far
remained motionless. With his eyes wide open and a

dignified posture shuffle, he begins to explain the difference. The bait has been taken.

According to Amara, Theravada and Mahayana Buddhism both share the same core beliefs and are devoted to the life and teachings of the Buddha. However, there are differences:

Theravada Buddhism hails from Sri Lanka, Thailand, Burma, Laos, Cambodia and parts of South East Asia, whereas Mahayana Buddhism originated in Tibet, China, Taiwan, Japan, Korea, Mongolia and parts of South East Asia. The Buddha's teachings or scriptures are detailed in the Theravada tradition in Pali (Pali Canon). On the other hand, Mahayana is recorded in Sanskrit (Sutras). One thing they do have in common is the Four Noble Truths and The Eightfold Path. All of sudden, Amara stops and gently closes his eyes. In the words of Bugs Bunny, 'that's all folks'.

Half-Sister returns to her monastery experience and starts to explain all about the meditation and chanting that took place in the Dharma Hall. She tells us of the special energy she experienced in her meditation, and how she could have meditated for hours. Finally, to the delight of The Bookshelf, she recounts the Dharma Hall filled with the sound of chanting in the unfamiliar language of Pali. Wandering Mind is quick to remind her not to forget to tell everyone about the harmonies they created. Harmonies might be stretching things a bit here - more like random humming due to not understanding the words. Still, it sounded fun. Half-Sister wisely declines the offer to re-live the experience. The Bookshelf, who is in full detective mode now, asks Amara directly if they meditated and chanted in the same way in his monastery. He has very little choice but to answer. Amara continues his thread of comparing Theravada and Mahayana Buddhism by explaining that Theravada is predominately Samatha (calming meditation), and Vipassana (insight meditation). Mahayana, meanwhile, has a greater emphasis on mantras and chanting, especially in Tibetan Buddhism. Conveniently for Amara, the storm clouds have passed and the sun has emerged. He doesn't need an invitation to end the conversation, and is quick to stretch and head for the back garden. Half-Sister would have preferred a little more time, but has had a successful fishing trip none the less. She is once again grateful to her trusted ally The Bookshelf. It is obvious that Amara is very knowledgeable in matters relating to Buddhism. The latest conversation has only deepened our suspicions that there is more to him than meets the eye. Further investigation will be necessary. Just as Amara reaches the dining room door, The Bookshelf lets rip with another pertinent question. Amara stops for a moment. You can almost see his mind considering whether he should answer or not. Then, with a shrug of his shoulders, he continues on his way. It is obvious he didn't want to tell The Bookshelf whether his monastery/palace was the highest placed building in the world.

Om Mani Padme Hum, or words to that effect

So far, The Bookshelf is keeping his council regarding his last question to Amara. He must have his reasons, so we will leave it at that for the moment. We are currently more interested in the sounds emanating from the living room. Jessica has been at it for a while now, and shows no sign of stopping. The Bookshelf, who is never short of a theory, thinks she has picked up on the word mantra from our conversation with Amara. After checking her data, she has come up with the Tibetan Buddhist mantra Om Mani Padme Hum. For some reason, she is now unable to stop. We have to say that it is a very catchy ditty, and we soon find ourselves all at it. Even Wandering Mind is chanting it, although she says it's making her sleepy. We only manage to stop the incessant chanting when Dad comes downstairs to see what Jessica is on about. He resorts to his favourite IT skill, and turns her off and back on again. That seems to have done the trick.

One thing we all agree upon is that it is a powerful mantra. Half-Sister asks The Bookshelf to tell us more about it. It does not require a board meeting to rule out asking Jessica; that would be classed as a high-risk strategy. The Bookshelf informs us that a mantra is a phrase of words and syllables. It is recited over and over again to aid concentration on a beneficial state of mind. This is to protect the mind from negative states, or in the case of Wandering Mind, to aid sleep. Mantras are believed to have special spiritual powers. We will need to investigate that possibility. One thing we can confirm is their addictive powers - the whole house feels like it is on mantra alert. In Sanskrit, 'man' means 'mind', and 'tra' means 'tool', therefore 'mantra' equals 'mind-tool'. That makes sense. Mantras apparently help to settle down the mind and maintain mindfulness. Now that can't be a bad thing. The particular mantra we were chanting, Om Mani Padme Hum, translates as 'The Jewel is in the Lotus'. It is repeated over and over to invoke the loving and unconditional qualities of compassion. Half-Sister likes the idea of this mantra and suggests we incorporate it into our practice, as long as we can stop it once we have started. It could also be useful for the moggy meditation group and their current issues; no doubt Half-Sister will test that theory. Wandering Mind has now awoken from her mantra-induced coma and is currently imagining levitating mantra-chanting moggies circling the skies. A gruesome sight indeed, and a thought not to be pondered upon.

At the next moggy meditation session, Half-Sister starts by introducing the mantra. Why wait? After all, if it succeeds in invoking compassion and settles the mind in preparation for meditation, it has to be a win-win. Everyone is in attendance, including Amara, who is in his usual spot under the bamboo. Half-Sister begins the mantra. "Om Mani Padme Hum, Om Mani Padme Hum". Over and over she chants the sacred words. Now the unfamiliar Sanskrit words are proving challenging for the group. The Ginger One, always one to throw himself into things, is currently chanting something that sounds similar to Om Mani Padme Hum. Give him his due, his tail is definitely swishing in time - it's like a stripy ginger metronome. The Siamese, on the other hand, has just about got it sussed. His oriental roots have obviously come in handy. As for the rest, well, it can best be described as random humming with the occasional right word dropped in. That aside, they are thoroughly enjoying themselves. The Wheezy Twins have found another gear, and are rocking from side to side in time with the rhythm of the words. Extra medication for them tomorrow. The White One has forgotten about his black-tipped tail, a result in itself. Amara, meanwhile, is yet to join in. He is simply sitting in his dignified posture with his eyes closed as the party rocks on around him. Half-Sister continues on, but slows the pace a little. This appears to have worked, as the mantra becomes clearer. They are getting the hang of it. Finally Amara begins to chant the mantra. His pronunciation of the Sanskrit words is immaculate. Half-Sister eases back a little so that Amara takes the lead. All of a sudden, thanks to Amara's diction, the mantra begins to flow. Om Mani Padme Hum indeed. They have cracked it; the sacred words reverberate through the bamboo, into the back garden, and swirl their way into the woods. All that is left to top things off would be the Buddha at the base of the bamboo to get up and start boogying. Needless to say, this does not materialise because, as usual, the Buddha is unbothered by such goings on. The rest of us, however, are intoxicated by the hypnotic mantra, and find ourselves chanting along enthusiastically. The Book-shelf is waggling his pages in time with the mantra, and Jessica is at it again. There are more purple spins flying around the living room than a disco ball at a night club. Eventually, and probably just in time, the mantra begins to abate. The chanting gets slower and slower, and then naturally draws to a close. Half-Sister then moves into today's meditation. It's dignified postures all round as slowly each member of the group closes their eyes. She is just about to begin, when out of the corner of her eye she notices a tear slide down Amara's cheek and fall to the earth below.

Reflections under the bamboo

Half-Sister's ingenious plan to extract information from Amara worked perfectly. However, we think he is wise to us now, and we will need to put our thinking caps on for round two. The Bookshelf is hard at work researching and piecing together all the information we have so far. He will only share his findings with us when he is certain of the facts. It's the way he operates. Om Mani Padme Hum still reverberates around the house and garden on occasions. Every now and again the moggy meditation group request a rendition, and party time starts all over again. Unfortunately, Jessica is yet to find the off switch. If Dad has gone out of the house it's a long day. I have noticed that Half-Sister is spending more and more time under the bamboo. I have seen this behaviour before. She is weighing things up, and if history repeats itself, there will be an announcement soon.

8

A Trip to the Countryside – anxiety goes on holiday

I long for the countryside. That's where I get my calm and tranquillity - from being able to come and find a spot of green.

Emilia Clarke

If the Buddha had been with us today he would surely have agreed with Half-Sister that, without a shadow of a doubt, this is the spot.

HALF-SISTER'S SPANIEL INTUITION HAS been activated early this morning. She tells me to pack my tennis balls as we are heading to our little house in the Northumberland countryside for the weekend. How she knows this is a mystery to me; nevertheless, I will follow her instructions to the letter, as she has never been wrong before. Sure enough, an hour later the bags have been packed and Dad is loading the car. Uncanny. The journey takes approximately one hour and twenty minutes. This is my current pukeless record - any longer and I will let one rip.

With the car fully loaded, Dad heads to the back garden to make sure Amara has enough food to last him the weekend. He is currently sitting under the bamboo and appears to be deep in conversation with Half-Sister. She has a glint in her eye and is shuffling her paws - a sure sign she is up to something. As Dad reaches the back garden, Half-Sister bounds to greet him and in the process appears to accidently stand on Amara's paw. He lets out a little squeak that is more like a mouse than a cat, and proceeds to limps a couple of times as he follows Half-Sister. It was nothing really, and he has stopped limping already. However, eagle-eye Dad has spotted the limp, and has gone to report it to Mum. Half-Sister throws a wink at Amara and tells him he will feel better after his holiday. A few minutes later, Dad returns with an old cat box that has been in the garage for eons. He has obviously decided to take Amara along to keep an eye on his imaginary limp. As the cat box and Amara head for the car, Half-Sister nods at its new resident. A squashed-up Amara tries to replicate the nod, but only succeeds in banging his head.

As for Dad, he is completely unaware that he has fallen victim to yet another Half-Sister cunning plan. This is not the first time Dad has been conned, and it will certainly not be the last. To celebrate her success, Half-Sister announces that we are all going on holiday, and that The Bookshelf and Jessica are in charge of the house while we are away. We can only hope that The Bookshelf doesn't say anything that triggers Om Mani Padme Hum, as it will be three days before it stops.

As the car pulls off the drive and heads down the street, we pass The Ginger One and The Siamese stretched out on the bonnets of two parked cars. If they knew that Amara was on the back seat of the car en route to a weekend break with Half-Sister, we may have had our first two cases of spontaneous feline combustion. We are travelling in Mum's car today, although Dad is driving. This is normal for us spaniels. Dad has a shiny new car and is reluctant to transport two hair shedding, part-time puking spaniels on the back seat. We don't mind - Mum's car is cosy, and has a pretty quilt on the back seat. It has a lovely design, but we are not sure if that is due to all the dog hair. Amara, meanwhile, seems comfortable enough, although he is a tight fit in the cat box. Due to his previous occupation as a ship's cat, we would assume he is a relatively good traveller. Time will tell. After a short while, Half-Sister's indicator navigation system informs us that we are turning onto the motorway and heading north. It's a straight road for the next hour. Time for a kip.

I am awoken from my slumber by an unsubtle change in road conditions - something akin to Mum's washer on spin cycle. This signifies the last seven miles of our journey. It's a bumpy ride, and I can feel the sea that lives in my stomach getting a little choppy. Dad has a theory that slowing down helps alleviate my travel sickness. In my opinion he would be better off just putting his foot down. Half-Sister knows the signs of impending regurgitation, and has edged further into the corner of the back seat. Amara sits helpless in his cat box having been reincarnated into a sitting duck. This will be a close one.

The humiliation of respraying the back of the car and guests is avoided in the nick of time. Everyone breathes a collective sigh of relief as the car turns into the country park where our little house is situated. There are lots of these little houses scattered about, all different shapes and sizes. One thing they all have in common is a veranda - ideal for perusing the countryside and its inhabitants. As we drive towards our house we can see that there are umpteen dogs doing just that. You can't help but notice that there is more than a smattering of spaniels on patrol. Eventually, we reach our house and are up on our paws as we pull into the drive. Dad starts unpacking the car, whilst Mum, carrying Amara, opens the front door. We are let loose on the veranda whilst Amara is allowed to explore the house. A quick bark from Half-Sister and his limp miraculously returns. A further bark swiftly follows - this one ensures he limps on the right foot.

Once everything is unloaded and safely packed away, a family meeting ensues. It is unanimously decided by

Mum and Dad that Amara should stay in the house as he may get lost in unfamiliar territory. Dad has brought one of those indoor travelling toilets that cats use. Its amazing what you find in our garage. Half-Sister is biding her time, as she has every intention of busting him out when Mum and Dad vacate the premises. The house that is, not the toilet.

After a spot of lunch we soon find ourselves outside on a walk around the country park. It's a great place, with lots of wide open spaces, and a copious amount of trees. There are secluded places where you can sit and meditate, or just reflect on the wonder of nature. Situated within the grounds are three ponds with a multitude of ducks, geese, water hens and swans. As for the rabbits, it's like the pub emptying five minutes before the match is due to start. They are everywhere, and running in all directions. They are fast little blighters, but have nothing on the hares. If the hares slowed down a little we might just be able to make out what make of motorbike they are riding, as surely nobody can run that fast! If all this beauty was not enough, we also have a farmers field to play in. You can run for miles, and miles. What more could a spaniel ask for?

When we return to the house, we are surprised to find that Amara has ventured outside and is currently sunning himself on the veranda. Half-Sister suggests that as we are all together, a meditation and dharma talk would be a good way to end the afternoon. As we are in the countryside, she is going to talk about what the Buddha said about meditation and nature. Very apt.

When the Buddha left his comfy palace in search of enlightenment, he spent most of his life living in forests, woodlands, and parks. This natural setting was the catalyst for his eventual awakening, and the venue for most of his teaching. He understood the connection between nature and meditation practice, hence his instruction to meditate in a forest at the base of a tree. It can be most helpful to meditate outdoors - what better setting is there than to be sitting on the earth surrounded by the sounds and smells of nature? It's like a new tennis ball versus an old one that's been thrown around the garden - one only knows the inside of a box; the other has lived life to the full.

Just like our old pal The Bookshelf, the Buddha also liked his metaphors. He would often reference nature in his teachings, using phrases such as 'like the rising sun' and 'a flowing stream' to emphasis a point when teaching. You can find metaphors such as 'concentration is like a peaceful pond' 'spiritual maturity is like entering the stream' and 'like a lotus rising from muddy water' scattered throughout the Buddha's teachings.

Meditating in nature can also provide us with important lessons, including seeing the impermanence of life and how everything is constantly changing. Half-Sister ends the dharma talk with a reading:

You do not have to be good.
You do not have to walk on your knees
for a hundred miles through the desert, repenting.

97

You only have to let the soft animal of your body
love what it loves.

Tell me about despair, yours, and I will tell you mine.
Meanwhile the world goes on.
Meanwhile the sun and the clear pebbles of the rain
are moving across the landscapes,
over the prairies and the deep trees,
the mountains and the rivers.

Meanwhile the wild geese, high in the clean blue air,
are heading home again.
Whoever you are, no matter how lonely,
the world offers itself to your imagination,
calls to you like the wild geese, harsh and exciting —
over and over announcing your place
in the family of things.

Wild Geese
Mary Oliver

Amara looks in reflective mood after Half-Sister's
dharma talk and reading. Either that or he is yet to use
his litter tray. We leave him to it as Mum is cooking in
the kitchen and has carrots. She is also talking on her
mobile phone. We position ourselves in anticipation;
everyone know she can't multitask.

Evening arrives with a stunning sunset as we all
snuggle up on the sofa, or in one of the many little hidey
holes that are scattered around the house. Amara finds a
suitable spot and curls up as only cats can. We are in our

usual position - the one that looks like we have been assassinated. It's raining outside, and the raindrops are banging on the roof as if they want to be in. In the distance we can hear the occasional rumble of thunder, accompanied by the odd flash of lightning that lights up the skyline. However, like the Buddha in the back garden we are unbothered by inclement weather, although I do sometimes feel the urge to look for a duck when the thunder arrives. Thinking about home has reminded us that The Bookshelf is currently home alone, apart from one purple-spinning, constantly talking virtual assistant. We would love to be a fly on the wall at this very moment. Just before I drift off to sleep, I ask Half-Sister what the plan is for tomorrow. She gives me an upside-down wink and tells me we are going in search of a suitable tree.

A tree in the forest

'The Dharma that I taught is just a handful of leaves. The Dharma is actually all the leaves in all the trees.'

Buddha

In the morning we are awoken by the sound of Dad staggering out of bed. He will no doubt take us outside for some necessities before preparing our breakfast. Strange as it may seem, it is exactly an hour later than we normally get up at home. At first we were confused as to why we always sleep in when we stay at this house, but upon reflection the answer became apparent. No timed central-heating, no springer spaniel activation system. Once Half-Sister has shaken the over-snoozyness out of her ears, she begins to explain the plan for the day. As is customary on these countryside excursions, Mum and Dad will hit the pub for lunch. They are of the opinion that we are troublesome when it comes to food. As if. We think they are misguided in that judgment and should take us along, although there is a rumour circulating that Half-Sister once cleared a pub of crisps in the

Lake District. She was only a puppy at the time, and certainly not the wise spaniel she is now. Anyway, the doubt has been placed so we will be left behind, just as Half-Sister visualised it last night. What she didn't visualise was the after-effects of last night's storm and the intensity of the humidity this morning. This is a blessing and the answer to our prayers - as they say, The Universe moves in mysterious ways. I have been briefed by Half-Sister, and once again I am happy to report that I have been promoted on the spaniel career path; in fact, I have been head-hunted. I will explain further. Due to the temperature today, Dad has left a window slightly ajar to keep us all cool. He does this at home if it's a hot day and he is cutting the grass in the back garden. I am banned from the garden on grass-cutting days, as I am renowned for lobbing a tennis ball under the lawnmower so he has to stop and throw it. On occasions he is not quick enough, and the beloved tennis ball is massacred in front of my eyes. It's a horrible sight, but soon there is another unwilling participant to take its place. Dad is at a loss as to how I escape from the house, but really all that is required is a leap to the windowsill, a bum wobble in the right place, and bingo. Half-Sister is banking on this impressive skill to manoeuvre our escape into the woods today. From decoy, to undercover agent, to escapologist, not only am I being promoted, but the words are getting bigger too.

As lunch time approaches, Mum and Dad don their coats and head for the car. My moment has arrived. I am just about to put my backside into gear when

Half-Sister puts the brakes on. It looks like Amara has no intention of going anywhere, as he is still ensconced in his hidey-hole. Fear has gripped his good eye (who knows what is gripping his dodgy one). Seeing as this whole expedition is for his benefit, Half-Sister will need to use all her persuasive powers or the mission will be aborted. It appears venturing into an unfamiliar place with wide open spaces is a step too far. Half-Sister reminds him that we will be there with him all the way. She adds that if his concern is around him only having one life left, he should consider the possibility that his thinking around this subject could be incorrect. In fact, as far as Half-Sister is concerned we all only have one life left and need to live that life to the full, or we will waste it. Out of the blue, Wandering Mind turns up and suggests the safest bet would be for us all to just stay at home. She is holding the hand of Fear, who is nodding like one of those dogs you put in the back of your car. Half-Sister ignores them and takes a different approach. She reminds Amara about the time he surprised us with a quote from Thich Nhat Hanh. He is a wise man, and perhaps if he was here with us right now he might share another quote to inspire us to be brave and face our fears. She recites the following:

"But a cloud can't be born; it has come from the water in the rivers and oceans, and dust and heat of the sun have helped create it. A cloud can never die; it can only become rain or snow. A piece of paper can't be born; it's made of trees, the sun, the cloud, the logger and the worker in the paper factory. When we

burn a piece of paper, the paper is transformed into heat, ash and smoke; it cannot be reduced to nothingness. Birth and death are notions that cannot be applied to reality."

There is a long pause as everyone looks reflectively at each other. The prolonged silence remains intact until Wandering Mind, in her wisdom, decides to let go of the trembling hand of Fear and announces that it is time to go. It seems Thich Nhat Hanh's reading has instilled a new-found determination in a most unlikely place. Slowly and purposefully, Amara stretches and rises to his paws. Game on.

Fortunately my bum-wobbling escapology skills have lost none of their edge. As soon as I put the rear end into action, I find myself through the window and sitting on the grass outside. Half-Sister swiftly follows; Amara is next. For one tantalising moment it looks as if he has changed his mind. Half-Sister and I hold our breath; then, to our relief, he arches his back and glides through the air. Once we have our bearings, Half-Sister guides us along the hedge that runs around the edge of the field until we reach the first of the three ponds that adorn the country park. It looks as if we are going on a tour of the gardens before our search begins for a suitable tree. We linger awhile at the pond, taking in the beautiful plants and flowers that circle the water. Today the occupants include swans, water hens and ducks, plus their offspring that are all at different stages of development. Keeping a low profile, we continue on until we reach the impressive derelict castle that is situated in the middle of the park. Amara seems to be captivated by the building, and shares his thoughts with Half-Sister. What has captured his attention are the trees growing inside the castle. I agree that they are fascinating, especially their branches, stretching out of the windows like giant tentacles. Before the castle was built, there would probably only have been trees. Sadly they would have been chopped down to make way for the construction. I would imagine people lived in the castle, and for all we know there may even have been a cat employed to keep down the mice and rats. For whatever reason, they are all gone now, so the trees - who have waited patiently for years - have returned to reclaim the land. Everything is impermanent; everything changes. Half-Sister nods in agreement. Most of that makes sense; however, in those times cats were associated with witches and dodgy magic. Today jobs are hard to come by for our feline pals. Some only work one night a year for treats, and even then it's only the black cats. It is more likely that the people in the castle had a dog to keep out the cats, but I won't tell him that. Leaving the castle behind, we edge further along the hedge until we eventually reach the farmer's field. It looks like the farmer has only recently cut the hay as there are big bales all over the place. Half-Sister pauses for a moment as we consider the best way to navigate the field. There are two options to contemplate: we could follow the path that surrounds the field, or we could leg it straight across. If The Bookshelf were here, he would no doubt say that we could circumvent the field, or travel as the crow flies. Half-Sister sides with the crows, so we head off in a straight line. Everyone is keeping to the plan and walking across the field as if the route had been drawn with a slide rule. However, as we reach halfway there is a very familiar sensation arising in my legs. It's one I know very well - well enough to know you can't fight it. It's a feeling that can lie dormant for days, but as every spaniel knows, once it arises it will not be denied. The zoomies have arrived. Wandering Mind surfaces and quotes a line from the Borg in Star Trek: '*Resistance is futile.*' I'm gone. By the time Half-Sister and Amara reach the other side of the field I have done twenty laps, including circling every hay bale twice in the process. I eventually reach my destination and, complete with a newly acquired lolloping tongue, re-join my comrades. There is no ticking-off from Half-Sister; she knows the zoomies are a force to be reckoned with. Amara on the other hand is totally perplexed by the whole episode. Some things are best left unexplained.

After a short break to catch my breath, the journey

continues, with Half-Sister leading us through an area of recently planted trees. They are all wearing their plastic trousers to stop the deer nibbling at them - it seems to be working as they all look healthy. Up ahead, we can see the forest stretching out as far as the eye can see. I wonder how Half-Sister will pick a suitable tree with so many to choose from? After a short while, we reach the edge of the forest and decide to rest for a few minutes. Amara is holding up well considering how far he is from the house. That said, he is staying very close to Half-Sister. After all, in his eyes she is responsible for keeping his solitary life intact.

Peering into the forest, it certainly looks a bit gloomy in there. The trees are quite dense and the undergrowth is thick. The trees are surrounded by the usual array of green and brown ferns in a variety of shades, their delicate leaves swaying in the gentle breeze. The Bookshelf, who is a bit of an authority when it comes to ferns, told me that the leaves of a fern are called fronds. He also informed me that there are no boy or girl ferns, just ferns. I thought that was a shame - it's a bit pointless calling your pet fern Mable or Albert. Where the light is able to pierce the canopy of branches, a ray of sunshine makes its way to a fern like a spotlight shining on a pop star. It's as if its time has come, and it is about to burst into song. Needless to say, this doesn't happen, and we are left to wonder what its androgynous voice might sound like. Some trees have fallen over, and have become homes for plants and no doubt furry woodland creatures. Although it's imposing and slightly scary, it's also a beautiful scene and very, very silent. There is no postponing the inevitable as the time arrives for us brave souls to venture into the depths of the forest in search of Half-Sister's tree of meditation. Wandering Mind materialises and decides she will give it a miss, choosing instead to stay at the edge of the forest and play 'I spy' with Fear until we return. As we take our first tentative steps, we are delighted to discover that there is actually a path. It's small, but it's definitely a path. Like intrepid explorers, we weave our way through the forest - or perhaps, more appropriately, like Lassie trying to find her way home. Half-Sister is leading the way; Amara is in the middle and yours truly is entrusted to bring up the rear, so to speak. It seems like we have been walking for miles when suddenly Half-Sister stops. Right in front of us there is a clearing, and in the middle of the clearing there is a huge tree. I'm not sure what kind of tree it is, but it's a magnificent specimen. If the Buddha had been with us today he would surely have agreed with Half-Sister that, without a shadow of a doubt, this is the spot. I ask her exactly how she knew this wonderful meditative oasis was here. Much to my surprise, she tells me she had no idea it existed - she just followed her nose and the Universe provided.

Half-Sister instructs us to find a suitable place at the base of the tree and to take up our dignified postures. We duly oblige, although I am beginning to think someone should keep an eye open. After all, we are in the middle of the woods. Although I have not been instructed to do so, I have taken it upon myself to volunteer. My experience in the look-out department surely makes me an ideal candidate for the job. As I suspected, we will be partaking in a sitting meditation - Half-Sister's favourite, and very appropriate in the current circumstances. Although the Buddha sat under the bodhi tree all those years ago in order to attain enlightenment, today our aim is to alleviate Amara's anxiety. The meditation begins ...

The Breath

We begin the meditation by bringing our attention to the fact that we are breathing, and are encouraged by Half-Sister to bring awareness to the breath as it enters and leaves the body. This is so we get a sense of where the breath is most prominent. For me, that is definitely at the end of my shiny black nose. Half-Sister then instructs us to do our best to not control the breath - allowing it to just breathe itself, and to be however it wants to be. I open one eye and have a quick scout about; everything seems as it should be, a picture of stillness, apart from the rustling wind. Half-Sister and Amara are like statues: motionless. I close my eye and join them. We are advised to bring a friendly curiosity to our observation of the breath, and to follow each breath from the beginning to the end. If we are distracted by thoughts, sounds or sensations, we are to gently bring our attention back to the breath. I don't know about the others, but as Wandering Mind is currently engaged in a marathon game of 'I Spy' with Fear, things are pretty quiet here. With my breath flowing with the trees and my paws firmly planted on the earth, it's as if the whole forest is breathing and we are all meditating together.

The Body
We have been following our breath for what seems an eternity. I have never known Half-Sister guide such a long period of meditating on the breath. She no doubt has her reasons. Eventually, she expands the meditation to include the body and any sensations that are arising. After all that time meditating on the breath, there is an overriding sensation that has arisen from sitting on the forest floor. Half-Sister, using her famed intuitive skills, gives instructions on how to deal with intense sensations if they arise. She explains that we could choose to move or stay with the sensation. Alternatively, we have the possibility of using the breath to breathe into the sensation and soften around it. I consider all that, and choose to open one eye.

Sounds
The next instruction from Half-Sister is to expand our attention to listening - an awareness of sounds. We are to let the sounds come to us rather than chasing after them. Although difficult, we are also encouraged to resist labelling or judging the sounds, perhaps just letting them come and go. All of a sudden there is a beautiful sound circling the ferns and trees. This is followed by a subtler sound that is quieter, but similar in tone. I know that we are to refrain from labelling, but I suspect this is the wind and our breath. I also know

in this moment why the Buddha encouraged us to meditate in nature.

Thinking

Although Half-Sister spends a long time exploring sounds, I could have stayed with listening even longer. I find myself drawn back repeatedly to the sounds of the forest, but reluctantly move to thinking. The guidance is to attend to thoughts as they arise and pass. If I find myself lost in a thought, I am to return to observing the thinking process as soon as I notice. I know what to do - I have practised the sitting meditation under the bamboo with Half-Sister on many occasions. Today, all my thoughts are fixated upon being in the woods, and how peaceful and tranquil the experience is.

Emotions

Time to move on again - this time we are bringing awareness to emotions. I have noticed that sometimes thoughts trigger emotions, and they are not always pleasant, but today they are simply contentment and happiness. Half-Sister reminds us that we can return to the breath if a difficult emotion arises. However, there is no need for the breath in this moment as everything is high on the tickety-boo scale. One emotion that does arise is concern; this is brought on by a sudden urge to see how Amara is getting on. I open one eye and have a peep. Nothing - just a dignified posture and his eyes closed tight.

Choiceless Awareness

For the remaining part of the meditation, we are to let go of all objects of attention and simply sit. I immediately find myself transported back to the breath and the wind moving through the forest. A strange thought arises in my mind that there is actually no difference between the wind and my breath. They are one. In that moment, the Buddha's words that everything is connected makes perfect sense. Half-Sister will be proud! Wait until I tell The Bookshelf about this - he will say I have had an epiphany. And I didn't even go to the vets.

Slowly, we open our eyes. It takes a little while to adjust to the light, which has changed. Everything appears darker and there is a shadowy tint to the forest. Either the sun has gone in, or we have been meditating for an awfully long time. Not only that, but the dim light is making it difficult to see the path we followed. Half-Sister takes charge as we set off in the general direction of home (we think). One thing I have noticed as we weave our way through the undergrowth is that Amara seems very calm, cool and collected. Bearing in mind we could become lost at any moment and have to spend the night in the woods, this is a tad surprising. We trudge on until Half-Sister suggests we take a quick break to catch our breath. Amara suddenly pricks up his ears and tells us to listen carefully. At first I don't hear anything, only the panting and chuffing of two dogs and a cat. Then, in-between the Wheezy Twin impersona-tions, I hear it. It's faint, but it's unmistakeable. 'I spy

111

with my little eye something beginning with ...'
Salvation.

When we reach the edge of the woods, Wandering
Mind is beside herself with worry. She has been dreaming
up every mishap known to man, woman and dog. She
has been ably assisted by Fear, who seems to have a gift
for the unfortunate.

There are no zoomies this time as we head back across
the farmer's field and into the park. The derelict castle
looks eerily like a horror movie set as the light fades and
the moon casts a shadow through the broken windows.
Up ahead there is another light. It's moving back and
forth, and is heading towards us at pace. Contrary to
Fear's belief that it's a one-eyed giant rabbit, its turns
out to be Mum and Dad with a torch. Busted.

Following a much appreciated tea, we settle down on
the cosy sofas and return to our familiar upside-down
view of the world. There is no reprimand for legging it
into the woods, as they are just pleased to see us back
safe and sound. The only dressing-down is reserved for
Dad for leaving the window wide open. Oops.

In the morning, everything is packed away in the car and
it's time to make the return journey home. There has been
no time to discuss the meditation in the woods experience,
so we will save it for later and include The Bookshelf in the
inquiry. That's if he has survived the home alone with
Jessica encounter. All that meditating, calmness and tranquillity has had its effect, as on my journey home there is
minimal chuffing and zero pukeyness. Upon arriving home,

we greet The Bookshelf with traditional spins and barks. As always he is happy to see us, and flutters his pages in delight. I cannot hold it in any longer, and so enthusiastically tell The Bookshelf all about my epiphany in the woods. From the dining room, a purple spin with a hint of red emerges. Jessica then asks The Bookshelf if he would like her to define epiphany, or will he do it himself? He tells her he has it covered, but thanks her for asking. She flashes another spin and then replies, "OK dear". I look at Half-Sister, who currently has a matching tongue hanging out. What shenanigans have been taking place here while we have been away?

Reflections under the bamboo

So much has happened that it is difficult to know where to begin. I suppose the obvious starting point is Amara and his anxiety - or rather his lack of anxiety. Ever since he returned from meditating under the tree in the woods, he has become more and more adventurous. Every day he ventures further and further afield. It is apparent that his confidence is returning, and the old swaggering Amara is back. Half-Sister is pleased with his progress, and impressed with my epiphany, as is The Bookshelf. Such was the impact of meditating under the giant tree that everyone has kept their thoughts to themselves. I think we are all still reflecting and giving thanks that we found the teachings of the Buddha in this lifetime. Finally, there is the conundrum that is Jessica and The Bookshelf. Whatever transpired in our absence remains a secret. If you ask The Bookshelf, he simply says, "We have an arrangement". We dare not ask Jessica.

9

The Buddha's Footsteps, Suspicious Minds, and Prayer Flags in the Wind

People take different roads seeking fulfilment and happiness. Just because they are not on your road, doesn't mean they have gotten lost.

Dalai Lama

Amara, who seems to be our authority on all things relating to Tibet, arises from his radiator-induced slumber and proceeds to explain the Tibetan Year of the Earth Pig.

TODAY, WHEN DAD ASKS Jessica what year it is in the Tibetan calendar, she proudly announces that it is the year of the Earth Pig. We have no idea why he asked her that particular question as we are not privy to the workings of his mind, which is just as well. However, it makes a nice change from the morning weather forecast which is the usual announcement. Talking of pigs, the pot-bellied variety that turned up in the field have since disappeared. Perhaps they have upped sticks and legged it back to Vietnam? We would like to think so. Amara, who seems to be our authority on all things relating to Tibet, arises from his radiator-induced slumber and proceeds to explain the Tibetan Year of the Earth Pig. He informs us that if you are born in the Earth Pig year you are regarded as being happy, organised, relaxed by nature and generally unaffected by criticism. Interesting.

Through the dining room window, we can see that Dad - who we must say has awoken in a very industrious mood - is currently carrying a variety of brightly-coloured square flags into the back garden. They are blue, white, red, green and yellow, and have strange symbols and peculiar writing on them. Amara, who has been watching with great interest and enthusiasm, suddenly declares that they are Tibetan prayer flags. We are fascinated to know more, and ask him to explain further. He is happy to do so, and judging by the expression on his face, he would have anyway.

He explains that the writing on the flags is a combination of symbols and prayers that are used to promote peace, wisdom, compassion and strength. This is splendid, as it's all the things we are currently studying and putting into practice. The Tibetan people believe that the wind will blow the prayers and mantras into the surrounding area, spreading goodwill and compassion. Excellent - this gets better by the minute. The flags might look a bit raggy and frayed around the edges, but this is intentional. When they are made, they are left unhemmed so that they fade and fray. This symbolises the inevitable passing of all things. Here we go again - no matter what you discuss, the issue of impermanence always seems to arise. As the Buddha says, there is nothing that is not subject to ephemerality. Half-Sister is enthralled by Amara's expertise and asks if the colour of the flags mean anything. It is not a great surprise to find out that they are, indeed, significant. Apparently blue signifies the sky or space, whilst white is for the air or the clouds. Red is for fire, and green is for water. Finally there is yellow, which is the Earth. Neither The Bookshelf nor Jessica were apparently aware of these facts. Of course, they are now, and there is no doubt the said facts will be regurgitated in the future, gift-wrapped in a purple spin. As the conversation ends, so does Dad's spiritual DIY. We are delighted to see that our very own Tibetan prayer flags are fluttering in the wind, sending peace, wisdom, compassion and strength into the garden, and over the fence into the woods. Everyone with legs and paws heads out into the garden for a closer look - even The Ginger One Next Door has vacated his position under the bed to take in the splendid spectacle. The prayer flags have been placed in a prominent position so that they catch your eye when you enter the back garden. We doubt this has been done intentionally, but they certainly deflect your attention away from Dad's half-painted fence.

As we observe the prayer flags doing their job, we notice that Amara has chosen to observe our new garden feature from on top of the garden fence. He is facing the wind, which is blowing his fur in a variety of directions. We can't help but notice that his coat is thicker and darker these days. His body, braced against the current of air, has bulked out with all the food Dad has been giving him, and all the mindful walks with Half-Sister have added muscle. He is no longer the scrawny patchwork quilt that emerged from the mist all those days ago.

The rest of the moggy meditation group arrive to join The Ginger One Next Door for today's meditation session. They all seem impressed with Dad's handy work, but from the look on their faces and the slight tilt of their heads, they seem to be deep in thought. My money would be on them trying to work out if Amara made his way to the top of the fence the traditional way, or in the unconventional levitating manner.

Half-Sister has decided that today's meditation session should be held under the Tibetan prayer flags, next to the little tree and the fern that live in the corner of the garden. The group form a circle and drop into their best dignified postures. They gently close their eyes to the accompaniment of prayer flags fluttering in the breeze. I do not need any words to describe Half-Sister's meditation today, as it is a silent practice. Needless to say it was a quiet affair.

When it comes to the dharma talk, Half-Sister throws a curveball and invites Amara to reflect on a topic of his choice. He ponders for a while, and then duly accepts her invitation. This should be interesting. We all wait eagerly for the title of Amara's dharma talk - none more so than Half-Sister. He eventually announces to the group that his talk is called 'The Buddha's Footsteps'. We are intrigued. Amara begins …

The Buddha was born in approximately 566 BC in the kingdom of Kapilavastu. That's a funny time - I would hazard a guess that it's just before six o'clock, and that BC means Before Clocks. I will ask The Bookshelf later. Anyway, on with Amara's talk. *Soon after the birth of the Buddha, wise men arrived and predicted he would become a Buddha. This didn't impress his Dad, the King, one little bit, as he had grand ideas that his son would grow up to be a mighty ruler. The Buddha eventually married a princess called Yasodhara, and was bestowed with riches so that he would not want to leave the palace. But despite this, he became disillusioned and longed to see the outside world. He would, on occasion, sneak out of the palace to explore, and it was on one such trip that he discovered a world riddled with sickness, old age and death. A wandering monk, who had given up all his possessions in order to seek an end to suffering, passed the Buddha, and in that moment his mind was set on following a similar path.*

Having made his decision, the Buddha left his kingdom and loved ones behind and became a wandering monk. He even went so far as to shave his head to show he had renounced his worldly life. I remember Half-Sister describing the monks at the monastery as having shaved heads - now I know why. I love it when pieces of the jigsaw come together. Amara continues ...

The Buddha called himself Gautama, and spent his time studying with wise men: however, none knew the answer to the Buddha's question of how to end suffering, so he continued on alone.

On a full moon in the month of May, the Buddha sat under the Bodhi tree and entered into a deep meditation. Just like us in the woods really. I'm beginning to think a trip to the groomer's would have been appropriate. Too late now ...

The Buddha promised himself that he would remain under the tree until he had found an end to suffering. During the night, the evil one called Mara turned up and tried everything to tempt the Buddha away from his virtuous path. When the struggle with Mara ended, the Buddha had realised the cause of suffering and how to end it. He had gained the wisdom and understanding to see things as they truly are. He had become the Buddha — 'the awakened one.'

For the next forty-five years, the Buddha and his followers travelled across India spreading The Dharma - the Buddha's teachings. He wisely advised people not to blindly follow his words, but to test them out and decide for themselves.

At the age of eighty, the Buddha sadly passed away. Although he left the world, his kindness and compassion remains till this day. The Four Noble Truths and The Noble Eightfold Path are at the heart of the Buddha's teachings, and the gateway to the end of suffering. So ended Amara's talk.

There is a period of silence before Half-Sister brings the session to a close. It is obvious to all in attendance that Amara certainly knows a lot about the Buddha. The moggy meditation group disperse as Half-Sister heads back to the house. Amara, on the other hand, has gone for a walk in the woods.

Half-Sister briefs The Bookshelf regarding the content of Amara's talk. He is impressed, and confirms that it is all correct in his book. We are particularly interested in the evil one, Mara, and are keen to hear the events of the Buddha's fateful night in more detail. The Bookshelf and Jessica compare notes and come up with the following:

As the Buddha sat in meditation beneath the Bodhi tree, Mara brought his most beautiful daughters to seduce Gautama. However, he remained in meditation.

Mara then sent vast armies of monsters to attack him, yet Gautama simply sat in meditation, untouched.

Mara claimed that the seat of enlightenment belonged to him and not a mere mortal. The monstrous soldiers cried out together, "I am his witness". "Who will speak for you?" challenged Mara. Then Gautama reached out his right hand to touch the earth, and the earth spoke: "I bear you witness." In that moment, Mara disappeared.

In the morning, Gautama realised enlightenment and became a Buddha.

That was scary stuff - it's just as well I kept an eye open when we were meditating under the tree in the woods. Although to be honest, if Mara had turned up with an army of monsters, I would have legged it pronto. I reckon Mara would have tempted us with carrots and gravy bones. That would have been a challenge. Talking about things turning up, Wandering Mind has just arrived with his new friend Fear. They reckon that the findings of The Bookshelf and Jessica totally justify their decision to stay at the edge of the woods. For once I am loathed to argue with them.

Half-Sister, who has been very quiet during the discussion, suddenly pipes up and suggests that we have missed one very important point. If we go back to our trek into the woods to meditate under the tree like the Buddha, we will find that there is something that doesn't quite add up. What a surprise! It feels like our lives have been dictated by a broken calculator since Amara turned up. All heads turn towards Half-Sister in anticipation of a revelation. I love it when a bit of poetry slips out by accident.

Half-Sister explains further. It is obvious to all concerned that Amara has considerable knowledge of the history of the Buddha. Where this information comes from we are yet to ascertain. However, one thing that is apparent is that this knowledge has not been acquired whilst he has been here. Therefore, he must have arrived with it already stored in his wise mind. Everyone nods in agreement, so Half-Sister continues.

Amara, although slightly resistant to the idea, willingly travelled to the woods to sit under a tree and meditate, just like the Buddha did all those years ago. He sat in his dignified posture, with his eyes closed tight, and didn't move a muscle. All the time he meditated, he was fully aware of what the Buddha experienced with Mara and his army of evil monsters, yet he appeared calm and tranquil throughout the practice. Fortunately for us, Mara has better things

to do than scare the living daylights out of two dogs and a cat. Nevertheless, my point is this: these are not the actions of a cat racked with anxiety and uneasiness.

The Bookshelf adds Half-Sister's conclusion to his ever-growing list of things about Amara that make little sense and are contrary to everything we currently know about him. For the first time since Amara arrived, The Bookshelf has an intuitive feeling in his wood that our unexpected visitor may have an ulterior motive, and that his story about his anxiety may not be all that it seems. In the next moment, Amara returns from his woodland walk. Even with one good eye, he cannot help but notice the suspicious looks that greet his arrival.

Reflections under the bamboo

The Tibetan prayer flags have settled nicely into their new surroundings. We would imagine that goodwill and compassion is now flowing around the garden and out into the woods. The said woods have become a favourite haunt for Amara recently; he regularly takes himself off into the trees for hours of contemplation. It is obvious that Mara holds no fear for him - an unlikely outcome for a cat supposedly racked with anxiety. This is only one of many contradictory behaviours that have manifested over the weeks. We wait with interest to receive The Bookshelf's report on the matter. In the intervening period, he has found a rather lovely poem.

Prayer Flags in Winter

against the snow
and the barren trees,
the gentlest breeze
moves the prayer flags.
white, red, green,
blue – they lift their skirts
just a little –
their frayed edges hang
like threads of compassion
into the world.
the slow morning sun
lights up the snow
and a bright empty space
for the whisper
of their tender secrets
to bless the air.

An excerpt from Moonlight Leaning Against an Old Rail Fence:
Approaching the Dharma as Poetry

Paul Weiss

As we sit under the bamboo at the end of another thought-provoking day, it suddenly dawns upon us that Wandering Mind has been strangely quiet of late. In fact, we can count on one paw the number of times she has made an appearance since we returned from our meditating in the woods experience. This is highly unusual for our little chatterbox pal; however, we are sure she will be in evidence soon. In the meantime, the silence in most conducive to contemplation.

10

Wandering Mind – and the shadow of Fear

Fear is the path to the dark side. Fear leads to anger. Anger leads to hate.
Hate leads to suffering.

Yoda

Half-Sister moves to the breath. Wandering Mind's fingers turn pink as the
healing powers of the breath have the desired effect on Fear.

TODAY THE SUN IS shining brightly and the sky is blue. There is not a cloud to be seen for miles and miles. The wind has dropped, and unlike yesterday's inclement weather, everything is peaceful and still. Even our newly acquired prayer flags are taking a breather, lining the fence like unfluttered butterflies resting on the lawn. The local moggies, meanwhile, are all stretched out in their respective gardens in what looks like feline yoga postures. Half-Sister and I have found the spot where the sun shines through the window, and are practising our springer sprawl in a pool of sunshine in the living room. Even Amara has left the comfort of the dining room and is currently upside-down under the bamboo. It's an idyllic scene in domestic pet suburbia - or is it?

It turns out that not everyone is living the stress-free life today. There is someone who is far from chilled, and desperately in need of Half-Sister's help. That someone is Wandering Mind, and her problem is Fear. Ever since the visit to the woods at the country park, she has been unable to shake the little blighter off. She is like a nagging shadow, constantly in Wandering Mind's ear. Always telling her to be careful, as this might happen, or that might happen. Wandering Mind is unable to move for Fear. Half-Sister will as always help, but a tiny little bit of us thinks Karma may have arrived early. Wandering Mind has been in our ears for years, although to her credit she has calmed down a great deal, especially since she came back from the monastery with Half-Sister. She still gets very excited when we have ideas, and can run riot with suggestions, though not all are practical to say the least. On the downside, she can be most unhelpful when things don't work out the way we expect them to. You can suddenly find yourself hit by an avalanche of negativity and doom-mongering. Half-Sister always sticks by her story that through it all, Wandering Mind is simply doing her best. Her motives are often driven by kindness, and at the end of the day she is simply trying to look after us.

Half-Sister consults The Bookshelf regarding an idea she has been formulating that will hopefully loosen the grip Fear has on Wandering Mind. Her cunning plan is to return Wandering Mind and Fear back to the outskirts of the forest by guiding them through a visualisation practice. After all, this is where it all began to go haywire. Maybe she can undo the knots of fear accumulated on that fateful day. It seems the endless rounds of 'I Spy' did very little to distract Wandering Mind and Fear from the terrors that inhabited their imagination. Half-Sister asks The Bookshelf if he has a suitable quote from the Buddha. As is the norm in this house he does not let her down:

How would it be if in the dark of the month, with no moon, I were to enter the most strange and frightening places, near tombs and in the thick of the forest, that I might come to understand fear and terror. And doing so, a wild animal would approach or the wind rustle the leaves and I would think, "Perhaps the fear and terror now comes." And being resolved to dispel the hold of that fear and terror, I remained in whatever posture it arose, sitting or standing, walking or lying down. I did not change until I had faced that fear and terror in that very posture, until I was free of its hold upon me ... And having this thought, I did so. By facing the fear and terror I became free.

Buddha

The Bookshelf asks Jessica if she has anything to add that might aid Half-Sister in her quest. There are several purple spins before a very matter-of-fact answer emerges.

All beings are not immune to fear. The Buddha taught that all beings experience anxiety. This comes from resisting the fact that their existence is impermanent. Fear is a mental event aimed at controlling a negative outcome. More purple spins emerge, and then silence.

Half-Sister requests that Wandering Mind be under the bamboo at mid-day tomorrow. She agrees, although Fear says if it's windy the bamboo could collapse and wipe us all out. We'll take that risk.

The following day we are pleased to report that the wind is mild. This has resulted in the bamboo still being intact and continuing to gently sway in the back garden. The guided visualisation will, therefore, go ahead as previously planned. At midday on the dot, Wandering Mind arrives. She is dragging Fear behind her, who seems beside herself with worry. It has obviously taken a great deal of effort for them both to keep the appointment with Half-Sister under the bamboo. Seeing the panic in their eyes, Half-Sister quickly reminds them of the Buddha's experience under the bodhi tree; hopefully this will stop them legging it in a trauma-powered sprint. She follows this up by suggesting that they do not react by taking unskilful action, but instead facedown the fear just like the Buddha did with Mara all those years ago. They are reminded that most of our moments are not fearful or anxious ones. In this moment, for example, we are simply sitting under the bamboo - all is well. This has the effect of calming them slightly, although Fear's grip on Wandering Mind's hand is turning her fingers white. Half-Sister sits them down beside the Buddha under the bamboo and instructs them to gently close their eyes. Fingers tightly entwined, they do just that, although Fear is concerned about the lack of light. After a few moments of grounding themselves in the present moment, Half-Sister moves to the breath. Wandering Mind's fingers turn pink as the healing powers of the breath have the desired effect on Fear. However, as Half-Sister instructs them to imagine they are back at the edge of the forest, the grip tightens and the white-knuckle ride begins.

A visualisation practice is no problem for Wandering Mind and Fear - their imaginations are fine-tuned from endless practice. No sooner has Half-Sister uttered the words then they are back at the edge of the forest in their minds, playing 'I Spy'. Although they have their eyes closed, their mouths are busy, and Half-Sister can hear every word. In a short while, the vehicle that drove Wandering Mind into the town of misery becomes very apparent. The agent of doom was none other than the game of 'I Spy', or to be more accurate, Fear's inter-pretation of it. Whereas Wandering Mind's version was delivered in the standard format with references to trees, clouds, rabbits and other mundane objects, it was obvious from the beginning that as a child, Fear had been given the Grim Reaper box set. By the time we emerged from our marathon meditation session under the tree, Fear had been through the whole alphabet in gruesome detail. Wandering Mind had been completely brainwashed, and was as a consequence, afraid of her own shadow.

Half-Sister continues the practice by guiding Wandering Mind and Fear skilfully to the sanctuary of the breath. Hand in hand, they breathe in and breathe out in perfect unison. After a short period of settling and calming, the practice then moves on to the observation of thoughts and emotions. This should be fun. Half-Sister expertly guides them through the process of watching thoughts and emotions as they come and go. As we have been told by Half-Sister on many occasions, everything is arising and passing - nothing is permanent. Thoughts and emotions are simply mental events that come and go, like clouds in the sky, or in Fear's case, ghosts in the night. Now initially, the desperation twins don't believe a word of this. Their tiny eyeballs are unable to see beyond their anxiety-ridden reality. However, slowly but surely, Half-Sister's determination and wise words begin to have the desired effect. The message is getting through. Just as the dreaded 'I Spy' game had programmed Wandering Mind, so the Buddha's words begin to unravel the illusion of fear. It is like moving from the ghost train on a stormy night to a trip to the seaside for an ice cream. As Half-Sister concludes the meditation, so two tiny hands slide apart. Wandering Mind is finally free from Fear.

She looks like she has just won the lottery. All of a sudden, Wandering Mind is back to her hyperactive best, even throwing in a little dance for good measure. However, her previous partner-in-gloom looks a forlorn figure. Fear is just standing, motionless, under the bamboo, like a child that has just lost her mum at the funfair. As far as she is concerned, her whole purpose in life has just vanished. Now Half-Sister, in her wisdom, had pre-empted this potential outcome. Taking them to one side, she begins to explain the reality of the situation. She starts by telling Wandering Mind that Fear is, in fact, her greatest teacher. Although Wandering Mind doesn't have a clue what Half-Sister is on about, at least the statement has succeeded in stopping Fear from sobbing all over the Buddha. As usual, he doesn't seem to be bothered in the slightest. Half-Sister explains further. Every time Fear arrives, you can ask her what lesson she is trying to teach you. You can choose to accept Fear, instead of fighting to be free of her. She can be an ally in your quest to make wiser decisions. Remember, she is on your side. When you tackle new challenges, take Fear with you, but don't let her stop you. Think of her as your wise council that will guide you through challenges and tricky situations.

Fear likes the sound of this, and you can see her confidence rising as the tears subside. Wandering Mind looks at Fear in a whole new light. Taking two steps towards her, she gently pats Fear on the back. Seeing the progress that has been made, Half-Sister reinforces the message with a reading:

AUTOBIOGRAPHY IN FIVE CHAPTERS

I walk down the street.
There is a deep hole in the sidewalk.
I fall in.
I am lost… I am hopeless.
It isn't my fault.
It takes forever to find a way out.

I walk down the same street.
There is a deep hole in the sidewalk.
I pretend I don't see it.
I fall in again.
I can't believe I'm in the same place.
But it isn't my fault.
It still takes a long time to get out.

I walk down the same street.
There is a deep hole in the sidewalk.
I see it is there.
I still fall in… It's a habit.
My eyes are open.

I know where I am.
It is my fault.
I get out immediately.

I walk down the same street
There is a deep hole in the sidewalk.
I walk around it.

I walk down another street.

By Portia Nelson

Side-by-side, Wandering Mind and Fear head off into the afternoon sun, Half-Sister's wise words ringing in their ears. Somehow we think it will take a little while before Wandering Mind is brave enough to take her by the hand.

Half-Sister, satisfied that her mission has been accomplished, heads back to the house for a well-earned drink. Halfway across the garden she notices Amara sneaking out from behind the bamboo and heading off into the woods. Interesting.

If a tree falls

In the evening we gather in the dining room as usual. It's been an exhausting and emotional day. Amara has come in from the woods and is stretched out next to The Bookshelf. Half-Sister, who has had a busy day, is lying under the table doing her fireside rug impersona-

Side-by-side, Wandering Mind and Fear head off into the afternoon sun,
Half-Sister's wise words ringing in their ears.

tion; yours truly is in a similar pose, but inverted. The Bookshelf decides that due to the intensity of today's activities he will pose a question for some gentle discussion. In the time it takes to turn a page, he comes up with the following - a philosophical thought experiment regarding observation and perception. The man who originally posed the question was Dr George Berkeley. 'If a tree falls in the forest and no one is around to hear it, does it make a sound?' Well, it's a topical question given all the time we have spent in the company of trees; however, it's laced with the potential for a ponder-induced headache. I decide to take the role of an impartial observer. Amara rolls over and accidently bangs his head on the radiator. With a quick shake of his head, he then takes up a position similar to that of a curled- up python, and closes his eyes. Looks like this one is down to Half-Sister and The Bookshelf, with the occasional comment, no doubt, from Jessica. Half-Sister, who can't resist a debate, opens the discussion. 'Sound is vibration that is transmitted to our senses through our ears and recognised as sound at the nerve centres. The tree falling will produce vibration of the air - if there are no ears to listen, there will be no sound.' The Bookshelf considers this and formulates his reply. 'If a tree falls it will most certainly make a sound, even if no one is around. The tree will displace air molecules as it falls and create sound.' Touché. Half-Sister smiles - she likes these discussions, and is happy to be proven wrong, if she is indeed wrong. In the hope of reaching some kind of conclusion, the question is posed to Jessica. An answer is soon on its way: "If by sound you mean compressions and rarefactions in the air which result in physical disturbances that cause the falling tree to propagate the air with audio frequencies, then the answer might be yes." The ponder-induced headache stirs from its slumber. The Bookshelf is happy to agree to disagree. Meanwhile, yours truly, who has remained silent throughout, suggests we could leave Dad's phone in the woods on record. As no comments are forthcoming, I close my eyes and leave them to it. The Bookshelf draws the discussion to a close. However, the final words are uttered by Fear, who has been hiding under the table. "If a tree falls in the forest, run."

Reflections under the bamboo

Wandering Mind and Fear's new relationship continues to blossom. Occasionally they ask Half-Sister to revisit her teaching, just to keep them on track. After the trauma-ridden episode of 'I Spy', we are now wary to play the game, even after the Grim Reaper version has been put safely away. In future we may risk it, but only with The Bookshelf and Jessica. Finally, we come to the question regarding the falling tree. I have to report that the issue remains unsolved. In fact, it would be accurate to say that everyone is now past caring, apart from The Bookshelf, who will ponder it until eternity. Just as he did with the Tibetan prayer flags, The Bookshelf has unearthed another gem of a reading, this time in keeping with our tree theme. Half-Sister is intrigued as to why we are suddenly getting poems rather than his usual scientific approach. We have a theory - a purple spinning theory.

A Fallen Tree

Who will dance with the wind now that you're really gone?
Who will catch the sun's rays on the hot summer morn?
Who will slow down the gust when it's out of control?
Who will dilute the air that's toxic to my soul?
Who will speak to the clouds about sending the rain?
Who will shelter me from the storm and soothe my pain?
Who will stand in the rain when others hide away?
Who will provide a place for little birds to play?
Who will catch my rain drops before they touch the ground?
Who will keep luxuriant grass from turning brown?
Who will present me a fruit for my morning dish?
Who will nourish my eyes and satisfy my wish?
Who will fix this huge hole in the soil of my heart?
Who will give me comfort now that we are apart?

Howard Simon

11

Do Cats Actually have Nine Lives? – a ginger mishap

> I've lived nine lives… and this one is the worst.
>
> *Grumpy Cat*

The next morning, The Ginger One Next Door returns from the vets sporting a blue bandage and a glakey look.

THE TALE OF WOE begins to unravel one rainy morning. Everything in the garden and beyond is soggy, muddy and weighed down with water. Even the prayer flags are too wet to flutter - they just hang there like spaniel's ears after a damp walk. It had started raining at teatime yesterday, and it is still tipping it down at this very moment. Most sensible sentient beings are either in the house, or tucked up somewhere dry in the forest. It is one of those days when, due to inactivity, curiosity kicks in, and you become interested in things that would normally pass you by. For instance, you can watch the sky for hours on end looking for a sign of blue, or observe the antics of a spider making an intricate web in the window. You can study The Bookshelf filing his books in alphabetical order, or ask Jessica questions that you hope she cannot answer. If you happen to be one of The Wheezy Twins, you can tick off the passing minutes by counting your steroid tablets. However, it appears that The Ginger One Next Door chose to do none of these things. He, in his wisdom, decided to pull an all-nighter.

It is Half-Sister who spots him first, to say he is wet would be an understatement to say the least. If you can imagine a ginger biscuit that has suffered a dunking accident you would have an accurate description of his fur. Head down, ears flat, he battles the elements as he slinks precariously along the garden fence. Just looking at him makes everybody shiver - even the radiator turned itself up.

Now when it comes to balance, The Ginger One is as surefooted as the best of them, but in these exceptionally stormy conditions he is struggling to keep it together. Not only is he like a sponge floating in the bath, but the fence is drenched and treacherous under paw. All of a sudden, and contrary to our expectations, the unexpected happens. One minute he is there, the next minute he is gone. Not only that, for the first time in his life, he doesn't land on his feet. The soggy mishap has everyone on their paws and stretching their necks to see outside. Concern etched on our faces, we peer out of the window. Worry begins to rise in our hearts as we scan the garden for any sign of movement; however, not enough for us to venture outside for a closer look. After what seems an exceptionally long time, we finally spot him slowly rising to his paws. By the look of him, he has either found a bottle of Jack Daniels behind the fence, or his fall was broken by landing on his head. Wobbliness personified, he staggers towards the back door of his house. With one giant effort he topples through the cat flap and lands on the kitchen floor. His body spread out in an ever-expanding ginger puddle, he lays motionless. Even The Siamese, who had eaten The Ginger One's tea and slept in his bed overnight, looks anxiously on. Time for the vets.

The next morning, The Ginger One Next Door returns from the vets sporting a blue bandage and a glakey look. His eyes, looking very similar to those of The Siamese, peer in both directions at once. In other words, the lights are on but there is nobody home. According to The Siamese, he is to have complete bed rest and is not allowed out the house in case he gets lost.

As we eagerly await the reappearance of our ginger pal, The Bookshelf decides to pass the time by flicking through the First Aid manual and reading up on neurosurgery. Jessica aids the waiting process by quoting cat concussion symptoms to look out for; these include trouble walking (we can tick that one off) and unresponsiveness. Interestingly, the definition of unresponsiveness, according to The Bookshelf, is not responding when someone calls your name, and staring into space for an unusually long period of time. We think there would be a very long waiting list at The Bookshelf's neurosurgery hospital were he to build it in the back garden.

Eventually, The Ginger One is released from house arrest. Still sporting his blue bandage, he ventures out into the garden for the first time since his unfortunate accident. Everyone, eager to make sure he is back to his old self, is watching his every move through the dining room window. The Siamese, who was ejected and sent back to his own house during the recovery period, skips into the garden, delighted to see his partner in crime. Much to his surprise, The Ginger One completely ignores him and continues on his merry way. Eventually he makes it to the top of the fence were he settles in for a long stare into space. His little head seems to be moving from side to side as he looks intently into the woods. It's as if he is trying to work out just where he is. Of course, this process of recognition has not been helped by a strange cross-eyed creature dancing in his path. Wandering Mind thinks that a first glimpse of The Siamese would make you query what planet you were on, never mind which garden. The Bookshelf, who has been observing and taking notes, suddenly produces a freshly-printed appointment card. Where did that come from? He carefully fills in the date and time, and in capital letters completes the section marked diagnosis: MEMORY LOSS.

In the coming days, it soon becomes evident that The Bookshelf is spot-on with his diagnosis. The Ginger One Next Door remembers zilch - in fact, he doesn't even know he is The Ginger One Next Door, or a cat for that matter. He is basically a blank sheet of paper. Much to our disappointment, Wandering Mind's splendid idea of telling him he is a chicken has been vetoed by Half-Sister on compassionate grounds. After yet another emergency board meeting, The Bookshelf's motion that we start by introducing ourselves and inviting him to join the moggy meditation group all over again is unanimously passed by all present. Half-Sister volunteers to start the rehabilitation process and duly introduces herself. She then invites him to the meditation session taking place in the afternoon. He has absolutely no idea who she is, and what he has signed up for, but says yes anyway. Joking aside, we are all very sad to see that The Ginger One Next Door has been reduced to a space-gazing, empty-nappered entity. None more so than The Siamese, who is very quiet, and is obviously pining for his buddy. However, it is not all bad news. According to The Bookshelf, cases of amnesia can resolve themselves at any moment. A further bang on the head could apparently reset The

Ginger One's database in an instant. In the end we decide to take the psychological approach. So, removing the hammer from The Siamese's paw, Half-Sister goes to work on designing a dharma talk specifically aimed at helping him regain his memory.

Half-Sister recruites The Bookshelf and Amara to assist in writing the dharma talk - after all, The Ginger One's future may be at stake here. It is through this collaboration of minds that a startling revelation is uncovered; he may have lost his memory, but in this moment he is seeing reality as it really is. He is currently locked in the ultimate beginner's mind, and for all we know, he could even be temporarily enlightened!

Half-Sister has already decided that a talk about beginner's mind might be helpful, and that the meditation should be a 'seeing' meditation. But Amara's suggestion that he must surely be seeing everything as if for the first time anyway has shed a whole new light on the situation. This is even more obvious when Amara defines beginner's mind according to Zen Buddhism:

There is a concept in Zen Buddhism known as shoshin, which means "beginner's mind." Shoshin refers to the idea of letting go of your preconceptions and having an attitude of openness when studying a subject. When you are a true beginner, your mind is empty and open.

One thing we can confirm is that his mind is definitely empty and open. Later in the afternoon, Half-Sister assembles the moggy meditation group under the bamboo. Everyone is present and correct, including The Ginger One Next Door, who is still wearing his newly-

acquired blue bandana. As instructed, everyone introduces themselves and then settles in for Half-Sister's
'seeing' meditation. Due to him having his hard drive
wiped, Half-Sister goes through the instructions for a
dignified posture in great detail. She would normally
have instructed the group to adopt a posture like the
Buddha under the bamboo. However, as he has no idea
who the Buddha is (or a bamboo for that matter), this
approach is deemed more trouble than it is worth. With
everyone suitably dignified, the meditation begins. As is
customary in meditation practice, the obligatory warning
is sounded regarding Wandering Mind and distraction.
Half-Sister then moves on to the breath, anchoring her
participants in the present moment. After a period of
mindfulness of the breath, the group are then instructed
to open their eyes. Everyone takes in the vista that
presents itself. Now, a seeing meditation sounds easier
than it actually is - how hard can it be to simply take in
the view? Trouble is, it's not observing that makes it
difficult, but rather Half-Sister's instruction to refrain
from labelling what you are seeing. Wandering Mind
loves this practice, and gleefully labels everything just for
the fun of it. You can tell she is in full flow by the
swishing tails of annoyance being displayed by the group,
although Amara only occasionally shifts his tail from side
to side. Conversely, there is one participant that has a
tail that is as motionless as a stalking python. It appears
that as the ginger mind has forgotten everything, there
is nothing to label. Nothing to get in the way, he is
simply witnessing the unfolding of reality, moment by

moment. Throughout the meditation, his tail remains as still as a discarded stick. When Half-Sister ends the meditation there is a cacophony of sighs, all apart from The Ginger One who mutters under his breath, "Easy peezy."

Beginner's Mind

"In the beginner's mind there are many possibilities, but in the expert's there are few."

Suzuki Roshi

All that is left in today's session is Half-Sister's carefully compiled dharma talk. The group as always are all-ears; none more so than The Ginger One, who is eager to discover what a dharma talk is. Half-Sister begins by explaining how thinking and beliefs get in the way of seeing things as they really are. Through past experience, the mind can become conditioned to see things a certain way; it thinks it's the expert. Beginner's mind is the willingness to see everything as if for the first time. She reminds them that every moment is unique and is full of possibilities. If we look at life with fresh eyes, every activity can be a meditation in itself. Half-Sister sums up by encouraging the group to bring beginner's mind to everything they do. The session ends with another quote from Suzuki Roshi, kindly provided by Amara:

"An open, beginner's mind allows us to be receptive to new possibilities and prevents us from getting stuck in the rut of

our own expertise. No moment is the same as any other - each one is unique and contains unique possibilities. Are you able to see the sky, the stars, the trees, with a clear and uncluttered mind?"

As the group disperses, Half-Sister hands The Ginger One her dharma talk notes, just in case he forgets today's session. He is most grateful, and looks inspired by the content of today's talk. With one graceful movement he leaps to the top of the garden fence. Just before he descends into his own garden, he defiantly launches his blue bandage into the woods.

In the coming days, The Ginger One, inspired by Half-Sister, embarkes on an intense period of meditation practice. Every time we see him, whether he is in his garden, the woods, down the street on the top of a car or on the front steps of his house, he has his eyes closed tight and is sitting in a dignified posture. His concentration is only broken by frequent trips to the vets to see if the lights have come on yet. Needless to say, his veterinary excursions have resulted in him striking up a renewed friendship with The Wheezy Twins, who are not adverse to the odd trip to the vets themselves. In fact, on his last visit they gave him the guided tour and proudly showed off their portrait hanging in reception. The Wheezy Twins are past masters at dealing with waiting room queues. Apart from instigating a breathing space, they have also been known to read their medica-tion leaflets and tick off the side effects to pass the time.

Unfortunately, despite the best efforts of the vet, there is still no improvement in The Ginger One's condition.

As time drags on, The Ginger One remains an enigma. He has run up an enormous bill at the vets, and his owners must be feeling the financial strain. If the lights don't come on soon, there will be no money left to pay the electricity bill. Everyone is most concerned and subject to extreme pondering - in fact, there is currently a waiting list for the bamboo. We are all wracking our brains in an attempt to come up with a plan of action - everyone but Half-Sister that is. At the next meditation session, The Ginger One Next Door sends in a sick-note via The Wheezy Twins. Yet another visit to the vets has produced an ideal opportunity for Half-Sister to share her thoughts with the rest of the group. All members are assembled; however, for the first time the bamboo is discarded in favour of the dining room. This is to enable The Bookshelf and Jessica to contribute if they see fit.

Half-Sister's opening statement has the potential to make this the shortest discussion in the history of discussions. After all our expectations that she had a cunning plan up her fur she simply suggests we do nothing. In her opinion, The Ginger One has simply been subjected to the law of Karma. The spiritual principle of cause and effect - in other words, the intention and action of an individual - influences the future of that individual. We should not interfere with the law of Karma, but rather let things unfold in whatever way they are meant to. Although we are sad that the old Ginger One may never return, we reluctantly agree that Half-Sister's philosophy is sound. The session is ended with a loving-kindness meditation dedicated to The Ginger One Next Door.

"You shouldn't chase after the past
or place expectations on the future.
What is past is left behind.
The future is as yet unreached.
Whatever quality is present
you clearly see right there, right there.
Not taken in, unshaken,
that's how you develop the heart."

The Buddha Gautama (Bhaddekaratta Sutta, MN 131)

Eventually the vet admits defeat and decides to let nature take its course, much to the disappointment of The Wheezy Twins, who had yet to show The Ginger One the cupboard where the steroids are kept. The bump on his head has now receded, leaving no visible signs of his mishap. Yet we all know that it is the space between his ears that is the issue.

Time passes by, and everyone does their best to create new memories for The Ginger One Next Door. He looks the same and is doing well, but as The Siamese says, he is not The Ginger One we remember, and he doesn't do what it says on the tin.

Now, Half-Sister has taken it upon herself to spend extra time with him in an effort to reacquaint him with the teachings of the Buddha. The thinking behind this theory is that something might just click in that little ginger mind and reboot his memory. All was going according to plan until Half-Sister told him about the Buddha becoming enlightened by meditating under the bodhi tree. It seems one of the side-effects from his injury is the tendency to become fixated upon things. We have witnessed this strange phenomenon in action. Recently, he spent the whole night staring at the moon after Wandering Mind told him that a man lived there, and that the moon was made of cheese. Today, after hearing about the Buddha, he has gone to meditate on a car bonnet and has informed us that he will not be returning until he is enlightened. Oops. At eleven-o-clock, The Ginger One begins his marathon meditation session. Eyes closed, dignified posture locked in, he takes his first mindful breath. Everyone, intrigued as to the outcome, takes up a vantage point and settles in. By the look on his face we might need duvets and a substantial supply of treats before the ordeal is over.

He obviously means business, as the day passes without a flicker of an eyelid. Half-Sister and I take turns to keep watch as night begins to creep in. The rest of the moggy meditation group have given up and gone to bed - only Half-Sister, Amara and yours truly remain on ginger watch. Throughout the night he doesn't move a muscle. He must surely be getting tired by now, as we are falling asleep and we are not even meditating. Our hope that his Mum would need her car and therefore shift his carcass does not materialize; she is obviously not at work today. At two-o-clock on day two, the rain begins to fall. It is heavy and bounces off the car bonnet, spraying The Ginger One in the process. Surely he cannot keep this up for much longer?

As we settle in for a second night, the rain continues to pour from the heavens. To make matters worse, the wind has now gotten up, causing the spray to hit The Ginger One right in the mush. Even though the weather has worsened, our intrepid friend has obviously taken a leaf out of the Buddha's book and remains unbothered. At this rate we might have the first ginger Buddha, as he is showing no signs of packing it in any time soon. Exhausted by our efforts to keep him safe and well, we succumb to sleep and close our eyes for a second. It is in that precise moment that he nods off and gently slides down the car bonnet. We are suddenly awakened from our minuscule nap by the sound of a ginger splat. For the second time in quick succession, he lay motionless in front of our very eyes. On closer inspection there appears to be no visible signs of life emanating from his water-logged body. The only movement detectable is the persistent wind and rain parting his fur in ginger patterns. His Mum, hearing the thud, arrives at speed and wraps him in a blanket. As she lifts him into the car, we can see the first sign of movement - a slowly rising bump that is announcing itself on the top of his head… vets.

Several days later, much to our relief, The Ginger One arrives back home. He is yet again sporting a blue bandage covering a substantial lump on his head. Ground-hog day. As he is carried from the car, it soon becomes

apparent to all concerned that he is not just back from the vets, but back to his old self. There is the familiar glint in his eyes as he winks at The Siamese, who has been waiting impatiently for his return. It seems, as mentioned by The Bookshelf, that another bang on the head can indeed do the trick. We think this approach falls firmly into Dad's 'switch-it-off-and-back-on- again' IT theory. Upon reflection, perhaps we were a bit hasty in removing the hammer from The Siamese, although Half-Sister would never have approved of the idea. The moggy meditation group welcome The Ginger One with open arms, as do we. At least now we can all get some sleep. We overhear his mum telling Dad that he has had a full medical, including a CAT scan (what else?) and has been given the all-clear. Karma has indeed returned to rectify the situation. As the saying goes, the Universe moves in mysterious ways.

Reflections under the bamboo

As we sit in our reflective oasis, everything in the garden seems rosy. The moggy meditation group is back to its full complement, and The Siamese has a spring in his step due to his ginger pal being restored to his former self. Half-Sister's wisdom has once again come up trumps. Today, she quoted Reinhold Niebuhr as a timely reminder to us all:

'Grant me the serenity to accept the things I cannot change, the courage to change the things I can, and wisdom to know the difference.'

Tonight we are back in the living room, and delighted to be tucked up cosy and warm on the sofa. In the dining room, The Bookshelf is reading 'Head Injury-A Practical Guide'. Sounds a riveting read. We would hope he never has to put this new learning into practice. However, as The Ginger One Next Door is currently staring at the moon from the top of the fence, it is obvious that some glitches still need straightening out. Better safe than sorry.

12

The Bookshelf's Theory

"It is a capital mistake to theorize before one has data. Insensibly one begins to twist facts to suit theories, instead of theories to suit facts."

Sir Arthur Conan Doyle, Sherlock Holmes

At precisely ten-o-clock, as predicted, Amara heads out into the woods and disappears into the shadows, his jet-black body vanishing in an instant into the inky darkness.

WHILST THE TRIALS AND tribulations of The Ginger One's karmic adventures have occupied our thoughts, The Bookshelf, although naturally concerned, has had other things on his shelves. Since the arrival of our unexpected visitor Amara, he has wrestled with a feeling of uneasiness. Although he likes Amara, and has had many a fascinating conversation with our mysterious guest, there is something about him that does not add up. The Bookshelf is a highly polished researcher; if there is a grain of truth or misleading fabrication to be found, he will find it. Half-Sister agrees with The Bookshelf - her spaniel intuition kicked in the day Amara arrived. She has given him the benefit of the doubt regarding his tale of anxiety, and has worked diligently to help him come to terms with the issue. However, she has misgivings about his colourful past, and his explanation of how he supposedly has only one life left. As always, Half-Sister will question everything. The Bookshelf, with the aid of his virtual assistant Jessica, has been meticulously collecting data on Amara. Between them they have logged all his elucidations and have researched every detail. Personally, I still think he is a bit scary, and will be back when I have looked up elucidations.

Lately there has been a noticeable shift in Amara's behaviour. He now spends less time in the house, and frequents the bamboo only occasionally. This is surprising given his attachment to the radiator. He has even taken to visiting the woods at night, and doesn't return until early morning. Although The Ginger One Next Door and The Siamese frequent the same woods every night, they are yet to bump into Amara. It's as if he vanishes into thin air.

All this reminds me of those intuitive moments that arrive out of the blue informing you that a visit to the vets is on the cards. There is no sound reason or information to back it up, but you know it's going to happen. Using the same ideology, I just *know* Amara is up to something.

With the flick of a page and a purple spin, a message arrives to inform us that the Amara report has been completed. The Bookshelf and Jessica are ready to share their findings. Tonight, as long as Amara heads out into the woods as usual, the candles will be lit for an all-night-sitting in the dining room. As the weather report is favourable and with no rain forecast, he should stay out until morning. By means of an additional precaution, the radiator has switched itself off to appear less alluring. This is the equivalent of Mum changing into her tatty old dressing gown after a night out.

At precisely ten-o-clock, as predicted, Amara heads out into the woods and disappears into the shadows, his jet-black body vanishing in an instant into the inky darkness. The Ginger One, despite still recovering from his ordeal, has volunteered to be the lookout. He is currently perched on top of the fence staring at the moon. He has assured us that if there's any sign of Amara returning, he will howl like a banshee. A mental image of The Ginger One Next Door howling at the moon, his ginger fur glistening in the moonlight, enters my head.

Maybe The Siamese would have been a more sensible option? Anyway, it's too late now.

Now that the coast is clear, The Bookshelf moves into action. He begins by spreading his meticulously prepared notes across the dining room floor. The urge to pick them up and start reading his findings produces spins of excitement; however, we know better than to interrupt The Bookshelf's presentation. Head positioned between our front paws, we settle in as The Bookshelf sets the scene. The candles are lit and the evening begins, the only interruption being a giant sneeze from Half-Sister. It seems we have lit one of Mum's smelly candles. Not to worry - Half-Sister's sneeze has sorted it. The scene bears all the hallmarks of a séance. I resist the temptation to ask if there is anybody there, just in case there is.

The Bookshelf opens the evening by taking us back to the very beginning; to the day Amara arrived. Revisiting that fateful day immediately poses a plethora of unanswered questions. First of all, he informed us that he had been searching for Half-Sister due to her reputation as a teacher. He conveniently left out where he had heard about her, and how he managed to find her. You don't just wander the Earth and suddenly stumble upon Half-Sister teaching the moggy meditation group in the back garden. Even a spaniel would have trouble sniffing that one out. The chances of it happening would be akin to being able to eat just one potato crisp, or taking a single bite out of a carrot and then giving the rest back to Mum for later. These things just do not happen.

Moving on The Bookshelf then broaches the subject

of Amara's name. Before he looks at the strange and potentially significant history behind it, he suggests that one burning question exists above all others. Just who gave him that name in the first place? Only Amara knows the answer to that one. If we had the answer, perhaps this whole mystery would unravel like a ball of yarn. We are left to ponder as The Bookshelf flips a page and continues his impressive reconstruction of events. The fact that Amara was a city in India where the Buddha happened to teach is an interesting coincidence. The ancient meaning of his name being an undying immortal god is also a contradictory and serendipitous finding. Listening to all these quirks of fate has got me thinking that there must be a point somewhere down the line when a coincidence metamorphoses into a fact. Just like a yellow tennis ball transforms from a thing of playful beauty into a busted yellow object that lives in the woods.

The next subject in the investigation, is in my opinion, the most puzzling and perhaps dubious part of this whole conundrum. I will be very interested to hear The Bookshelf's take on the reason Amara arrived. Somewhere deep down in the realms of spaniel intuition, his story of anxiety and ultimate life are just not ringing true. It appears that The Bookshelf is also unconvinced by Amara's explanation, and begins to itemize areas that are debatable and should be thoroughly investigated. Half-Sister, who has remained silent so far, simply nods her head. She does this when she is in serious contemplation mode, or when someone has done something she thinks is nonsensical. It is usually yours truly, or Wandering

Mind, or both, who are on the end of a Half-Sister nod.

The Bookshelf proceeds to list all the places Amara informed us he had spent time in. As is his want, he has meticulously recorded every word, and without delay quotes him chapter and verse:

"I once lived with a beggar in Calcutta in India, and had to shed fur because of the heat. I then stayed with a family in Genhe, Inner Mongolia, and had to grow a thick coat as it's one of the coldest places on Earth. Eventually I ended up in Tibet and was taken in by a friendly monk. I liked it there, but had to leave unexpectedly. Due to circumstances, I took a job as a rat-catcher on a ship and was nearly washed overboard in a storm."

As soon as The Bookshelf finishes, the questions come tumbling into my head. They are everywhere, and far too many to grab at once. I can see by the look on Half-Sister's face that she is thinking along the same lines. Impatiently, we resist the temptation to launch into dialogue, and allow The Bookshelf to continue. Thankfully Wandering Mind has arrived, and is eagerly collecting our thoughts so we can refer to them later. No doubt she will add a few herself. The first point of contention highlighted by The Bookshelf is regarding the vast array of countries that Amara has apparently lived in. Presumably he stayed a while in each one; therefore the question is, just how old is Amara? Then there is the monastery where he lived in Tibet. Amara delights in telling us about the monk who taught him to meditate. That would have taken a while. Perhaps the most intriguing part of the above statement is him having to leave Tibet unexpectedly. Why? The Bookshelf has a theory about that one, but is keeping his counsel for now. Finally, there is the stormy voyage on a ship where he was employed as a rat-catcher. Where was the ship travelling to? Presumably it ended up in England, where he began his journey north. Amara is willing to share information, but always leaves us to fill in the blank spaces.

Leaving the wise quotes that appear out of thin air, levitation lessons and pot-bellied pig recognition skills aside, it is his familiarity with Tibetan Buddhism that makes us sit up and pay attention. Looking back at his dharma talk, it is obvious that he has extensive knowledge relating to Mahayana Buddhism. His skill in translating that knowledge into a common language that the moggy meditation group can grasp shows a deep understanding of the subject.

This leads The Bookshelf nicely back to the beginning - back to the issue of anxiety. Half-Sister has done a sound job in guiding Amara through the trials and tribulations of coming to terms with his debilitating disorder. However, upon reflection, she has taught him nothing he did not know already. His talk revealed that he understood the essence of the Buddha's teachings, and the Buddha's journey to enlightenment. The Bookshelf is doing a fine job here - every time he unravels a little bit more of the mystery, Jessica lets fly with an admiring purple spin.

The next subject of intrigue and inspection is the journey through the countryside to meditate under the tree, just as the Buddha did in Bodh Gaya in India all those moons ago. At this point in the proceedings, Wandering Mind and Fear temporarily vacate the room. This is probably a wise move. We don't want Fear, who has been listening from under the dining room table, to have a flashback. All Half-Sister's hard work would be up the swanny, and she would need to start all over again to rectify the situation. After a short pause, The Bookshelf eagerly continues his hypothesis. If, as we suspect, Amara is very familiar with the Buddha's journey to enlightenment, then he was already aware of the Buddha's battle with Mara and his evil army under the Bodhi tree. Yet, even though he was supposedly wracked with anxiety, he still ventured into the woods. Not only that, he sat in his dignified posture and meditated all afternoon, without even the flicker of an eyelid. The Bookshelf shuffles his pages like a judge in a high court, and prepares to polish off his summing up. "Therefore, my friends, in my honest opinion, Amara's anxiety is a deception, and furthermore, I am of little doubt that he arrived with an ulterior motive." Half-Sister and I look at each other as only spaniels can. In all the years we have known The Bookshelf, we have never doubted his word. We are not about to start now. Just what is Amara's ulterior motive?

There is a period of silence as we take in The Bookshelf's impressive theory. Half-Sister eventually breaks the silence and confirms to The Bookshelf that she concurs with everything he has stated. She has had her doubts, but wanted to keep an open mind. When the time is right she will confront Amara, and hopefully discover his ulterior motive.

Although Half-Sister is confident in her abilities, I, on the other hand, think unravelling motives of an ulterior nature might be easier said than done. One of the things The Bookshelf omitted to mention was Amara's apparent aptitude for telepathic communication. I have been on the receiving end of this one, and it wouldn't surprise me if he wasn't already privy to The Bookshelf's theory and has decided to leg it. As The Bookshelf prepares to conclude his presentation and file away his report, Half-Sister asks her final question. Some time ago, when our doubts about Amara first began to surface, we held an impromptu interrogation session in the dining room. In that session we asked him some pertinent questions about his past. He was very careful with his answers, but did let one or two things slip. At the very end, as he was about to leave the room, The Bookshelf asked Amara if the monastery where he had lived in Tibet was the highest-situated building in the world. He didn't answer. Half-Sister had asked The Bookshelf at the time why he had asked such a strange question. He also didn't answer, other than to say he would get back to her when he had done more research. Half-Sister is asking again, and this time I don't think she will take no for an answer.

Reluctantly, The Bookshelf shares the train of thought that led to his mysterious question to Amara. Before he begins, he warns us that what he is about to share is probably the most illogical piece of information he has ever uttered. Wandering Mind returns - she is all ears.

Surely her award for illogical thinking cannot be under threat? The Bookshelf's irrational theory is as follows:

Amara informed us that he spent time in a monastery in Tibet, although he described it as much bigger that your average monastery. Half-Sister thought it sounded rather grand, and very unlike the monastery she visited with Dad. The fact that he was taught by a monk to meditate tells us that it was a monastery of sorts. It may also have been the venue for his indoctrination into the teachings of the Buddha, although he has not stated that this is the case. He has confirmed that the lineage of Buddhism was Mahayana - in other words, Tibetan Buddhism. The above gave us very little in the way of clues as to where this place actually is. After all, Tibet is a big country with a multitude of monasteries. However, when you add a further piece of information to the theory, the picture becomes a lot clearer. We await the clarity mentioned by The Bookshelf to emerge, because in this moment, we are looking at mud. Like a detective on the television, he draws out the suspense with a moment of silence before finally revealing the final piece in the Amara puzzle. "Amara stated that he liked it at the monastery, but had to leave in a hurry. I believe that the place Amara is talking about is none other than the Potala Palace in Lhasa, Tibet. The palace was the official residency of the Dalai Lama, until he had to leave in a hurry. He fled to India after the Tibetan uprising in 1959, where he remains to this day." There is stunned silence. Even Wandering Mind has nothing to say. It is Jessica who breaks the soundless moment with a purple announcement of monumental proportions. "The Chinese army invaded Tibet on the seventh of October 1950. After the Tibetan uprising in 1959, the Dalai Lama, fearing for his safety, fled to India, and currently lives in Dharamshala." Beyond belief does not begin to cover The Bookshelf's theory.

Although the theory appears to be outside the realms of possibility, Half-Sister, as always, has an open mind. After all, the Buddha could recall all his past lives, and was partial to the occasional levitation session. Some would say that is impossible, but Half-Sister knows better than to doubt the Buddha's word. She will revert to her tried and tested method of questioning everything until she truly believes it for herself. To do that, we will need to find Amara. It's time to round up a search party.

Reflections under the bamboo

Even though the bamboo is a place of reflection, today we have sat mainly in silence. Occasionally we have pondered just where to begin, but not for long. Half-Sister has said nothing - she is just sitting with her eyes closed. My thoughts are whizzing around faster than a contestant at the Olympic zoomies freestyle event. Although maths is not my strongest subject, I reckon that if The Bookshelf's theory is correct, then Amara is somewhere between seventy and one-hundred years old. Surely this can't be true? The moggy meditation group have been conscripted by Half-Sister, and are currently searching the woods. So far they have found no trace of Amara. His telepathic skills would make it easy for him to avoid them: however, their moggy intuition is telling them he is still here, somewhere. Half-Sister believes they will not find him because he is waiting for her. Looks like we are heading into the woods (or as I refer to it, the tennis ball graveyard). What concerns me is Half-Sister's cunning plan. Because we are not allowed in the woods alone, she has suggested we sneak out at night. Wandering Mind has agreed to accompany us, although she is currently back to holding the hand of Fear. Somehow I think we may be in for a night to remember.

> *"The impossible often has a kind of integrity which the merely improbable lacks."*
>
> *Douglas Adams*

13

The Truth is Revealed

Three things cannot be long hidden: The sun, the moon, and the truth.

The Buddha

The only thing that annoyed people was the dog's habit of getting as close to the Buddha as possible when he was about to speak. Because of this tendency, the dog was affectionately known as Right Nuisance.

AS ALWAYS WITH A Half-Sister cunning plan, the conditions for execution have to be just so. The blueprint for this latest initiative, surprisingly, requires yours truly to take on yet another role. This is becoming a familiar story. According to Half-Sister it's another step up the spaniel career ladder, although I am beginning to think this smacks of carrot and stick syndrome. My role in this grand scheme is that of a saboteur, whatever that is. The obvious way to find out is to ask Jessica, who, as usual, comes up with the goods. I could have asked The Bookshelf, but have a feeling I would have received the long answer, and time is of the essence.

Saboteur - *A person who deliberately destroys or obstructs something.*

As if to prove my point, The Bookshelf, hearing Jessica's reply, can't resist adding his two penneth. "Evidently, it's taken from the French word *saboter,* and really means to kick something with an old-fashioned wooden shoe." If Half-Sister's plan goes belly-up, I will be ordering an old wooden shoe from Amazon.

Out of all the cunning plans instigated by Half-Sister, this one is perhaps the most elaborate, and therefore requires *perfect* timing.

First of all, there is the small matter of the grass in the back garden. It is getting long and requires cutting. Hopefully today will be the day Dad gets productive with the lawnmower. This is an essential ingredient if the plan is to succeed. If we are to embark on our night-time mission to find Amara, we will have to enter the woods via the back gate of the garden. The gate is currently locked, but will be unlocked so that Dad can deposit grass cuttings in the woods. It will be my job to ensure the gate remains unlocked. This is where my role of a saboteur comes into play - I have to lob a tennis ball at precisely the right time and kibosh the mower. The precise time, according to Jessica, is five minutes past three. This is when it will start raining. Due to the inclement weather, a knackered mower and two spaniels spinning and barking in tandem, we are banking on Dad packing up at speed and forgetting to lock the gate.

The Bookshelf thinks it is a clever plan and has every chance of success, but he is curious as to which tennis ball has volunteered for such a potentially dangerous mission. The answer is that none of them have; in fact, most of them are currently under the sofa. After using my persuasive powers, a volunteer eventually edges forward. I tell him that as a result of his brave action he will probably have nothing more than a headache. However, if the worst comes to the worst, due to his courage and having lived a good life, he could be reincarnated as a football. That does the trick. With everything now in place, we await the thought to enter Dad's head regarding the state of the back garden. If the thought doesn't turn up, we are sure Mum will be forthcoming with one of her unsubtle hints. Either way, we will be in business.

At one thirty, Dad decides it is time to put the lawnmower in gear and tackle the back lawn. By the time he collects the mower from the garage, we are all positioned and ready for action. After the customary number of trips up and down the lawn, it is time to empty the grass cuttings. The back gate is unlocked and the process of mowing and depositing begins in earnest. Half-Sister and I nonchalantly stroll around the garden. Occasionally we join in with the depositing (if you know what I mean), just to make things look more authentic. Right on cue, the skies darken and the smell of rain is in the air. The tennis ball's moment has come. With perfect timing, the ball arrows under the mower, causing the emergency stop to cut in. There is a loud bang, followed by a wobbly tennis ball shooting out the other side. Looks like it's paracetamol rather than Match of the Day for my little yellow pal.

Dad looks down at the mower, then up at the dark sky, as huge drops of rain fall upon him. He immediately heads for the house - gardening is over for the day. Just as Half-Sister had predicted, his attention is focused solely on getting a broken mower, two spaniels and himself out of the pouring rain. In his urgency, he has forgotten to lock the garden gate. Bingo. According to Jessica, the rain is set for the day, so it's unlikely Dad will venture outside again.

Part one of the cunning plan has been activated successfully - we now have an escape route into the woods. Part two will take place this evening when darkness falls. Tonight is the perfect night, as Mum and Dad will be watching a movie on the telly. Not only that, but they will be on the vino. Mum always falls asleep,

The tennis ball's moment has come

and Dad will be engrossed in the film. On these occasions they always leave the back door open so we can pop into the garden for a wee; they will be oblivious to our absence until the movie ends. By our calculations, which have been verified by The Bookshelf, we have a three-hour window of opportunity.

Hello darkness my old friend

> *"Into the darkness they go, the wise and the lovely."*

> *Edna St. Vincent Millay*

Darkness falls like a blanket over a puppy's cage. We are ready. Wandering Mind and Fear have been briefed, and all that is left is for Dad to choose tonight's film. His fingers are zooming across the remote as quickly as a concert pianist playing 'The Flight of the Bumblebee'. Eventually, he settles on 'Star Trek into Darkness'. We hope this is not an omen. The description states that Captain Kirk leads a manhunt to a war-zone world to capture a one-man weapon of mass destruction. We will settle for finding a dodgy-eyed moggy in a dark world of trees. The film begins, the wine is poured, and two intrepid spaniels energise into the back garden and through the back gate.

The first thing we notice upon entering the woods is that it's not as dark as we first imagined. There is a full moon tonight, and everything is bathed in a milky glow. Unfortunately, the full moon has not helped the mood of Wandering Mind and Fear, who are currently discussing werewolves and bogeymen respectively. Half-Sister lifts the ghoulish vibes by telling us that only in the darkness can you see the stars. We all look up and stare in wonderment at the sparkling spectacle. The admiration of earthly phenomena is only broken when Fear reminds us that if we don't look down, we might trip and end up in the bed previously occupied by The Ginger One Next Door. It's a fair point, as there are no paths to follow. Without the moonlight, we might all be wearing blue bandanas by now.

On we trek through the undergrowth and trees, only stopping now and again as a rustle of leaves grabs our attention. There is no sign of Amara, just tiny creatures scurrying away as we approach. Unperturbed, Half-Sister ploughs on, guided only by her spaniel intuition. Looking back, we can see the lights of our house are getting smaller and smaller. Soon they will be gone, and it will only be our instinct that will help us find our way back home. Wandering Mind and Fear are predictably starting to query the wisdom of this venture. They are about to kick off big-time, when our attention is caught by two shiny lights protruding through the darkness. Half-Sister stops in her tracks and lifts a paw. Whoever this mysterious being is, it is certainly not Amara. Unless he has acquired a friend that is, because from what we can see there appears to be two of them. They are obviously on lookout patrol, because they are peering into the woods in opposite directions. Whoever they are, they are not moving, as Half-Sister edges forward to get a closer look.

Cautiously, she peers into the shadowy gloom, only to be greeted by a familiar face. It seems we have been deceived by the lights, which are, in fact, eyes. There is only one creature we know that can look in both directions at once. Our woodland guide has arrived in the shape of The Siamese. He winks at us in recognition, which only succeeds in making us feel dizzy. He informs us that he is yet to see Amara, but, as he knows all the unmarked trails in the woods, it should only be a matter of time before we stumble across him. Half-Sister invites him to lead the way - she still believes that Amara will find us, rather than us finding him. She may well be right. There is a collective sigh of relief from Wandering Mind and Fear, instigated by the fact that someone now knows where they are going. I am not so sure about that. How does The Siamese decide which way to go when he comes to a crossroads in the woods? After what seems like hours of walking around in siamese-y circles, we arrive at a large fallen tree that is blocking the way. It's a big tree, and its branches are covering a large area. By the time we navigate our way around or over the leafy obstacle, it may well be time to head back home. It looks like our journey is over.

As we prepare to turn on our paws, I notice Half-Sister has not moved an inch. She is standing motionless, with her right paw raised, and is staring straight ahead - it's her stalking pose. We used to see this a lot whenever she spotted a cat in the street; however, since she started studying and practising the Buddha's teachings, it has become redundant. Everyone turns their head to look in the same direction as Half-Sister. At first, all I can see is the fallen tree and broken branches. It reminds me of one of those puzzles where you have to squint to make a picture appear. Suddenly, I see what Half-Sister is watching, or rather what is watching us. Two golden eyes, one bright, one dull, and a body that is completely at one with the darkness. Amara!

Realising he has been spotted, he emerges from the tree debris. His black body is immediately immersed in moonlight, giving him the appearance of a spirit that has just reincarnated from a dead tree to a cat. He welcomes Half-Sister with a bow of his head - she mirrors the gesture, placing her paw back onto the ground in the process.   It looks to me as if Amara has acknowledged Half-Sister with the ancient greeting of *Namaste*.   The Bookshelf told us all about this customary Hindu greeting; it means *'I bow to the divine in you'*. It is patently obvious that whatever discussion is about to take place will be solely between Half-Sister and Amara. The rest of us will be merely bystanders. To create more space, we shuffle backwards, form a circle and take up a dignified posture. We know we are not going to meditate, but somehow everyone intuitively knows that, given the circumstances, it is the correct thing to do. The woods may be dark, but Wandering Mind is determined to take notes for The Bookshelf's archives. Her job is made even harder due to the fact that Fear has a tight grip on her hand, and is shaking like a jelly at a kids' party. I sit next to The Siamese, who has once again wrapped his tail around his body.

The thinking behind my logic might be a tad question-able, but it seems to me that Half-Sister was correct in her assumption that Amara would be waiting for us to arrive. He was hidden, but not that well-hidden. In the shadowy depths of the woods he could have easily remained secreted. I think he wanted Half-Sister to find him, and his telepathic talents will have informed him of exactly why we are here. If only The Bookshelf was present at this clairvoyantish extravaganza - his aptitude for detective work and attention to detail would have proved invaluable.

Silence falls upon the group as we await Half-Sister's interrogation. Amara, meanwhile, just sits in his now-familiar dignified posture. He looks like a contestant on Mastermind who knows all the answers. By the frown on Half-Sister's face, she is pondering where to begin. No easy task - the silence is deafening. Before she can compose herself, Amara breaks the uneasy stillness and speaks. He commences by referring to the Buddha after his enlightenment. Apparently the Buddha would, on occasion, recount stories of his previous lives. He did this to illustrate aspects of his teaching. They are called the Jataka stories, or put simply, they are the tales from the previous lives of the Buddha. In his previous lives, the Buddha was born as a human being, animal, bird and fish, both male and female. There are over five hundred and fifty Jataka stories. The consistent theme that runs through each one is the persistent effort to perfect the qualities that will lead to the attainment of enlightenment. Amara pauses, before telling us that the Buddha is not the only sentient being that has the ability to recall past lives. It appears that Amara has caught The Bookshelf's taste for the dramatic. All that time under the radiator has not been wasted. There is a break in proceedings as we take in Amara's last statement. In true Amara fashion, he has neglected to tell us who else can recall past lives. Looking at the expressions etched on the shadowy faces in the circle, it is obvious to all that he is referring to himself. Eventually our tongues are rolled back in, and after a period of intense shuffling back and forth, we are ready to continue. Amara then describes a series of recurring dreams. In these dreams, which he believes are his past lives, he can recall places and people in great detail. The beggar in Calcutta, the family in Genhe, Inner Mongolia, and the monk in Tibet are just some of the many vivid dreams that he can remember at will.

As we all sit aghast, Amara then plucks a thought right out of our heads. Wandering Mind didn't even see it coming. The vivid dream that has permeated Amara's mind has not been a dream from the past, but rather a dream set in the future. This recurring dream has been all about two spaniels, a group of cats and the teachings of the Buddha. He has seen it all in his dream - the statue of the Buddha, the swaying bamboo and a half-painted fence. The reason he is here is not anxiety. It is Half-Sister.

Amara apologises to the group for the mistruth. Spreading his front paws on the earth, he lowers his head. The act is so graceful and authentic that it feels like he is instantly forgiven. There are no comments from the group, and so silence prevails. Actually, thinking about it, if he had arrived and launched straight into a tale about dreams and past lives, he would probably still be in the vets to this day. Half-Sister, showing her usual compassion, nods to Amara as a sign of forgiveness. However, Wandering Mind is not so forgiving, and obviously doesn't appreciate being fooled. I am taking my lead from The Bookshelf, and keeping my counsel until I have all the facts. Everyone appears stunned by this latest development, and for one brief moment The Siamese even looked me straight in the eye. Half-Sister, meanwhile, shifts paws. She always does this when she is about to ask a question. Or is waiting for her breakfast. We all expect her to launch into a question about just why Amara has travelled presumably great distances to find her. Instead, she surprises us by referring back to the time he spent living with a monk in Tibet. Half-Sister is building up to something here. Amara begins by praising The Bookshelf and his virtual assistant. Looks like they were on to something all along. As The Bookshelf suspected, Amara did indeed live in The Potala Palace in Lhasa, but the monk in question was no ordinary monk. Half-Sister knows the answer before the words leave Amara's mouth. Our mysterious guest is none other than a reincarnated cat who lived with the Dalai Lama in Tibet. There is another short interlude as tongues are rolled back in again, this time with additional coughs and splutters from bits of earth. So, The Bookshelf's theory is on the money, right down to the hurried exit due to the Chinese invasion! Just wait till I tell him.

As I suspected, Half-Sister has one final question. She has been saving this one until last, although it will come as no surprise to Amara.

It's the question everyone has been pondering for weeks. The Bookshelf has wracked his pages for the answer but to no avail, whilst Jessica launched so many purple spins she almost made it to the mothership. Half-Sister has a feeling that the answer will send the final piece of the jigsaw spinning through the Universe. She takes a deep breath and a step forward, then in true Half-Sister fashion plants her eyeballs straight at him. With his telepathic abilities, he will know the question already; however, the drama is cool. Half-Sister asks her question, and as I half-expected, she wants to know where he acquired the name Amara.

Amara tweaks his whiskers and shifts his head from

side to side before re-engaging with his perfect dignified posture. He again begins with a reference to the aptitude of The Bookshelf to glean information, but we know this already. It appears that the name Amara is sometimes referred to as Amaravati. This is an interesting coincidence, as Amaravati is the name of the sister monastery connected to the monastery Half-Sister and I visited with Dad in Northumberland. With a wink of his dodgy eye, he tells us we should visit one day. We may well do that; however, as it is in South East England it registers dangerously high on the puke-o-meter. He confirms The Bookshelf and Jessica's findings regarding the city of Amara in India, and that the Buddha taught in the city. Half-Sister shifts from paw to paw - she is eager. As per The Bookshelf's research, his name indeed means immortal, undying, a god.

Amara then proceeds to tell us all the things we don't know, the things only he is privy to. As he begins to explain, Half-Sister's small piece of jigsaw drops its landing gear, and we all fasten our seat belts. By now we are beginning to become immune to information that stretches the bounds of possibility. Again and again, improbable facts have turned out to be the truth. Bearing this in mind, why should we doubt the next bit?

It turns out that in one of his many lives our mysterious visitor spent a great deal of time in the city of Amara listening to the teachings of the Buddha. He was so enthralled by the Buddha's teachings that he did his best to memorise every word. Since then he has followed the teachings diligently, and ventured forth on the road to enlightenment. Because he was such a frequent visitor to the grove that lay just outside the city, he was christened Amara by the Buddha's followers. It was a great honour for a previously un-named wandering cat. He stops talking for a while and looks up at the vast array of sparkling stars. It's as if the stars are his thoughts and he is gathering them before continuing. With a deep breath and a long sigh, he returns to his explanation. He is sure the Buddha would understand that the fabrication of anxiety was aimed at uncovering the truth. He realises he has broken the precept of false speech, but is willing to live with the karmic consequences.

Every day, he wandered down to the grove to hear the Buddha. Surrounded by the Buddha's followers, he would sit in the hope of gathering more wisdom. As the Buddha delivered his teaching, Amara noticed the continued presence of a dog. It sat, bolt-upright, ears gently flapping in the breeze, its face a picture of intense concentration. Occasionally it would shift from paw to paw, almost as a gesture of understanding. This was no ordinary dog that had wandered into the grove, foraging for scraps of food. This dog was a loyal follower of the Buddha. Amara discovered that the dog in question had travelled the land listening to the Buddha. Everyone loved it, as it was the epitome of kindness and compassion, and it was welcomed wherever it went. The only thing that annoyed people was the dog's habit of getting as close to the Buddha as possible when he was about to speak. Because of this tendency, the dog was affectionately known as Right Nuisance.

There is a collective intake of breath - it's like the beginning of a sneeze but without the shoo bit. Half-Sister's eyes have narrowed, and her ears are raised. She is wondering, like the rest of us, just where Amara is going with this. It turns out that Amara and Right Nuisance became good pals, and would spend hours discussing the teachings of the Buddha. When the Buddha moved on, Right Nuisance followed, and Amara lost touch with his kindred spirit. When he began dreaming of a dog instructing cats in the ways of the Buddha, his curiosity was aroused and his journey began. Eventually he found Half-Sister, sitting with the moggy meditation group under the shade of the bamboo. Who knows how long Amara has been searching for Half-Sister. When she asked him the question, he simply quoted the Buddha's take on being born human:

"Suppose that this great Earth had become one mass of water, and a man would throw a yoke with a single hole upon it. An easterly stream would move it eastward. A westerly stream would move it westward; a northerly flow would move it northward. A southerly stream would move it southward.

There was a blind turtle that would come to the surface once every hundred years. What do you think, would that blind turtle, coming to the surface once every hundred years, insert its neck into that yoke with a single hole?

It would be an extremely rare occurrence, that the

blind turtle, coming to the surface once every hundred years, would insert its neck into that yoke with a single hole.

So too, how extremely rare that one is born a human."

Buddha

Half-Sister seems to understand, and nods her head. The rest of us have booked appointments under the bamboo.

If Half-Sister is indeed the reincarnation of the Buddha's dog, Right Nuisance, she would know how to help a cat suffering from anxiety. She would know the teachings of the Buddha by heart, and she would be skilful in guiding her sangha in the ways of meditation. Above all else, she would be the epitome of kindness and compassion. Every day that Amara has been here he has been secretly testing Half-Sister, watching her every move and listening to every single word.

With that startling revelation, he concludes his discourse. Tomorrow, he will talk to Half-Sister one-to-one, under the bamboo.

Although we are disappointed, we understand that Half-Sister should be privy to Amara's findings in private. No doubt she will inform us later. The Siamese leads the way as we head back through the woods towards the house. Half-Sister has insisted that Amara sleeps in the house tonight. He does not argue, and looks relieved that the truth has now been revealed.

As we troop through the garden gate, we can see the

film credits rolling up the television screen. Perfect timing. Everyone settles in for the night. Wandering Mind hands her notes to The Bookshelf, Amara snuggles under the radiator and the world turns upside down as we inhabit the sofa. All is peaceful and serene. All apart from The Siamese that is, who has yet again ignored the fact that his house is just around the corner, and has instead decided to sing outside the back door of The Ginger One's house.

Reflections under the bamboo

You could argue that today has potentially been the biggest day in the life of Half-Sister. It may even have surpassed her trip to the monastery, or the time that, as a puppy, a carrot rolled off the kitchen bench. My intuition regarding Amara appears to have been proven right, although I will take back the fact that I thought he was scary. He is more mystical than scary, and only has Half-Sister's best interests at heart. There is currently very little need for a light in the dining room, as the glow of pride from The Bookshelf is illuminating enough. All he has done since we returned from the woods is to read and re-read Wandering Mind's notes. Jessica is very thrilled to have been his virtual assistant, and has told Wandering Mind that although she has more than enough information to return to the mothership, she is staying put. Eventually, The Siamese was let into the house next door, and by now he will have briefed The Ginger One of tonight's developments. I'm not sure how much sleep we will all get tonight, as tomorrow could be a very big day.

14

The Leaving

*"A farewell is necessary before we can meet again, and meeting again after
moments or a lifetime is certain for those who are friends."*

Richard Bach

*All that remains in the fading afternoon sun is Half-Sister, Amara
and the statue of the Buddha.*

AS WE ARE CURRENTLY in a period of extraordinary events, including the revelations of numerous lifetimes, telepathic communication and levitation to name a few, you would think that my ability to be surprised would be pretty low on the WOW scale. Not so. This morning, Half-Sister is up and ready before the activation of the central heating system. Unperturbed by the cold, Dad, thinking her barking is a signal that she needs an emergency trip to the garden, scuttles down the stairs at a rate of knots. Seeing that it is a false alarm, he feeds us, opens the back door and swiftly heads back to bed. No sooner is the back door open than Amara vacates the house for his morning constitutional in the woods. It seems Half-Sister will have to wait a little longer to discover the truth.

Today is a busy day - not only is it the day of Half-Sister's one-to-one with Amara, it's also moggy meditation day. Any more bookings for the bamboo and the Buddha will be selling tickets. However, we would hazard a guess that he is unbothered by all today's commotion. Ignoring her excitement, Half-Sister heads for the currently vacant bamboo and positions herself next to the Buddha statue. She is preparing for today's dharma talk, which is aptly entitled 'Reincarnation'. After a while, Half-Sister returns to the house to consult The Bookshelf. She is a stickler for detail, and wants to make sure she has left nothing important out of her talk. He reminds her that the Buddha and his disciples seemed to have gained knowledge of their past lives through the development of some sort of parapsychological ability, or you could call it extrasensory perception. Blimey - past lives, telepathic communication, levitation, and now parapsychological ability and extrasensory perception! What next? If the moggy meditation group teleport in today with their phasers set to stun, I will simply nod my head. Half-Sister is struggling to get her head around parapsychological abilities, and so asks Jessica for her input. There is a short silence whilst purple spins dance the dance of unlimited knowledge.

Parapsychology – *is the study of alleged psychic phenomena (extrasensory perception), as in, telepathy, precognition, clairvoyance, psychokinesis, telekinesis, and psychometry. It is considered as pseudoscience by many scientists because of a lack of evidence. Some even say that if parapsychological claims are true then the rest of science is not.*

No disrespect to Jessica, but I found that answer posed more questions than answers. I am just about to give up on the subject when Half-Sister comes to the rescue. She leans a little closer and asks me how I know when its teatime, or when Mum and Dad are due to arrive home? She questions that as I can't tell the time or even possess a watch, how do I know? I reply with my best confused look, as a gesture that Half-Sister should continue. Similarly, how do I know Mum and Dad are coming when the car is not even on the drive yet? I return to the look of confusion, this time with additional cross-eyes. Half-Sister nods her head in approval. I guess I am telepathic after all.

Morning comes and goes, and with no sign of Amara returning from the woods, Half-Sister turns her attention to teaching the moggy meditation group, who are beginning to arrive. Word seems to have spread about last night's revelation as The Ginger One Next Door, always first to arrive, has just lowered his head as if he was meeting The Queen. Half-Sister looks embarrassed, and is no doubt hoping he has not set the tone for the session. The Siamese slinks in next, having just arisen from The Ginger One's bed. He is well aware of developments, having been commissioned as the official sherpa last night. He did a fine job guiding us all through the woods in the dark – shame he couldn't make it to his own back door. The White One is his usual preoccupied self, and The Wheezy Twins missed everything due to a vets appointment. Half-Sister hesitates before inviting her group to take up their dignified postures and close their eyes. From the corner of her eye she notices a flash of gold, swiftly followed by the emergence of a black shadow that is winding its way through the woods. She waits as Amara takes his seat, closes his eyes, and sinks into his dignified posture.

Half-Sister begins by guiding the group through a body scan practice, allowing them the opportunity to explore sensations in their little furry bodies. The practice is longer than usual; Half-Sister will have a reason for this no doubt. Eyes are opened, bodies shuffled, as everyone settles in for Half-Sister's dharma talk on the subject of reincarnation. Now, a dharma talk on reincarnation is tricky. The Bookshelf has quite an array of books on the subject, yet I think even he struggles to get to grips with the theory behind it all.

Methinks Half-Sister will need to come up with some creative ways of explaining this one to the local moggies. Half-Sister tries the subtle approach, and asks the group if they are their bodies. Before they can answer, she follows up by asking them if when they have a sore paw, or in the most recent case, a sore head, they can simply ask their body to stop the painful sensation. There is a collective shake of the head. So far so good. Next, she asks them if they are their mind. Do they control their thoughts, or do they just arrive without an invitation? Again, a collective shake of the head. So, if they are not their bodies or their minds, who are they? Half-Sister pauses as she awaits the answer. Eventually, it is The Siamese that volunteers an answer. With his eyes on full beam, he proudly announces that they are cats. To make matters worse, the whole group nods in agreement. You can almost see the drawing board being wheeled out in Half-Sister's mind. The bamboo suddenly rustles in the wind; however, it's not the wind but rather Amara's laughter that is causing the leafy disturbance. If there is one thing you can say about Half-Sister, it is that persistence and determination are never in short supply. She very gently informs the group that the right answer was that they are simply part of the Universe - they are energy, or, as some people like to call it, stardust. 'Cats' is just the name humans gave them. They could have been called anything. Although the group is silent, you can see by the look in their eyes that the thought of being stardust appeals. Half-Sister continues at pace whilst the going is good. To reinforce her point, she quotes directly from one of her favourite books held by The Bookshelf for safe keeping:

"When this physical body is no more capable of functioning, energies do not die with it, but continue to take some other shape or form, which we call another life. ... Physical and mental energies which constitute the so-called being have within themselves the power to take a new form, and grow gradually and gather force to the full."

What the Buddha Taught
Walpola Rahula

Half-Sister recognises that this is not an easy concept to understand, and cannot be fully understood by reflection alone. For this reason, many schools of Buddhism emphasise that a meditation practice can enable the realisation that the self is an illusion, and with practice, the liberation from that illusion can be achieved.

Now, it may not appear obvious to the untrained eye, but deep down there might just be a glimmer of understanding arising in the moggy meditation group. No doubt Half-Sister will continue the discussion at a later date. Amara seems impressed with the final result, and nods in his now familiar manner.

After the session has ended, the moggy meditation group retire to consider the topic of reincarnation. All that remains in the fading afternoon sun is Half-Sister, Amara and the statue of the Buddha. As the wind rises, the branches of the bamboo begin to sway. It is as if they are motioning the conversation to commence.

Amara thoughtfully begins. Unexpectedly, he starts by reciting a quote:

"Because fate has a funny way of mending things back together. I mean, you are here and I am here, and we'll find each other again, that is, if that's the way it's supposed to be. So, if you believe, I believe."

R.M Drake

Half-Sister is intrigued, and rather sad. It seems to her that Amara has begun the conversation by announcing he is leaving. Life is full of surprises. Unfortunately, they are not always high up on the tickety-boo scale. He starts to divulge his findings regarding the Half-Sister—Right Nuisance conundrum. From a purely intuitive perspective, she reminds him of Right Nuisance. Then there is the strong will, the narrowing of the eyes and bouncing from paw to paw. These are all traits he recognises. The single-minded approach to the Buddha's teachings, especially the desire to question everything, is Right Nuisance to a tee. Her knowledge of the Buddha's teachings, in his opinion, could not have been learnt solely from books. It is too detailed, carries too much wisdom, and is delivered with a skill that could only have been learnt by listening intently to the Buddha. As if to confirm Amara's findings, Half-Sister narrows her eyes and shifts from paw to paw. All this, however, pales into insignificance compared to Half-Sister's embodiment of kindness and compassion. To embrace an anxiety-ridden stray cat, give it a home, and work diligently and skilfully to restore its state of mind, is truly impressive. Amara has studied Half-Sister intently - her knowledge of the Buddha's teachings, the teaching of the moggy meditation group, and her kindness in dealing with the many ups and downs of life. In his opinion, he is ninety-nine percent sure Half-Sister is the reincarnation of Right Nuisance.

Half-Sister takes a moment. Then, in true Half-Sister fashion, she narrows her eyes, flattens her ears and shifts her paws. Amara, having studied her for so long, knows what is coming. The good news, is that it is another Right Nuisance trait. The bad news is that the trait in question is perfectionism. Ninety-nine percent sure is not good enough.

Amara knew Half-Sister would not accept this - she has to know for certain. He shuffles a little closer, and then asks a very strange question. The question in question, as it were, is why does Half-Sister like stones? It's true - she does like stones. The bigger the better. She has carried them around the garden since she was a puppy. In answer to his question, Half-Sister doesn't have a clue why she likes them. All she can think of is that it's a habit. Amara winks. It might be a sign that Half-Sister is on to something, or he might just have something in his eye. He closes his eyes for a moment, before letting fly with another quote.

"There is life in a stone. Any stone that sits in a field or lies on a beach takes on the memory of that place. You can feel that stones have witnessed so many things."

Andy Goldsworthy

Amara begins to sum up and end the conversation. Half-Sister hasn't a clue what he is on about, and is shuffling her paws faster than a cowboy at a square dance. Finally, he sheds some light on the mystery. It appears that Right Nuisance also loved stones, and had one stone that was a particular favourite. She carried it with her everywhere as she followed the Buddha from city to city. There are symbols carved into the stone that only Right Nuisance would understand. Find the stone, and we will know for sure if Half-Sister is really the reincarnation of the Buddha's dog, Right Nuisance, or not. The only clue he has to the whereabouts of this stone is that it is closer than we think. Most helpful. Not. Apparently, he feels that the stone is situated somewhere in this part of the world, but the exact location eludes him.

With that statement, the conversation ends. Half-Sister heads back to the house to break the news that Amara is leaving in the morning.

The Bookshelf is first to react to the news. He is still enjoying the praise from having been on the right page with his Amara theory, but has mixed feelings regarding his imminent departure. He is sad that their little chats about the Buddha and the Dalai Lama will be over, but the thought of helping Half-Sister find her stone with so little to go on has excited his investigative tendencies. We have no idea how the radiator feels about it - one minute he warms to Amara, the next minute he goes cold on the subject.

Jessica simply agrees with The Bookshelf, which is the

norm these days. She is, however, quick to start the ball rolling by telling us a stone is a piece of rock. I don't think we could have lived without that piece of information. That was sarcasm by the way - not to be confused with a metaphor.

Wandering Mind is neutral, but wishes him well. Meanwhile Fear, his partner in trepidation, is just relieved that there is one less thing to worry about.

Half-Sister reconvenes the moggy meditation group and shares the news. They are visibly shocked and disappointed. After a shaky start, they have all taken to Amara. They share their feelings with Half-Sister and sit with their eyes closed, embracing their sorrow. All apart from The Ginger One Next Door that is. He has his eyes wide open, and a look of steely determination wrapped around his stripy face.

For the last time, Amara sleeps in the dining room next to The Bookshelf. For the second night in a row, Half-Sister does not sleep. At precisely 7am, the springer spaniel activation system switches itself on. It need not have bothered, as we are all wide awake. Dad trudges down the stairs and supplies everyone with a hearty meal. He is unaware that it's Amara's last day. If he had known, we are sure he would have given him extra food. Amara has not informed us of where he is going or why he is leaving. He will have his reasons, and we trust his judgement.

The bamboo is, once again, our refuge as we all sit in meditation bathed in the morning sun. Everyone is present apart from The Ginger One. We hope he has not had a relapse. Half-Sister invites Amara to guide the meditation, but he declines.

She seems a bit lost for words today, so it is no surprise that we simply sit in silence.

At the end of the practice, Half-Sister bows her head, and Amara mirrors the gesture.

Then, in the same way as he arrived, he takes his leave. The moggy meditation group are all sitting on the fence watching his departure, and we are happy to report that The Ginger One Next Door is with them. As the breeze arrives and ruffles his ginger fur, we notice that he appears taller than the others. In a parting gesture, Amara turns and winks his dodgy eye at a beaming ginger tomcat.

The search begins ...

Cast of characters

Narrator	Indi	Black/White Springer Spaniel

(Also known as Young Half-Sister & Yours Truly)

Half-Sister	Ella	Liver/White Springer Spaniel
(Right Nuisance)	The Buddha's Dog	Unknown
Amara	Charlie	Tom Cat
The Bookshelf	Himself	Wooden
Jessica	Herself	Cylindrical
Wandering Mind	Herself	Various
Fear	Herself	Various
Dad	Gary	Human Being
Mum	Kathleen	Human Being
The Ginger One	Pedro	Tom Cat
The Siamese	Charlie	Tom Cat
The White One	Max	Tom Cat
The Wheezy Twins	Frodo and Elron	Tom Cats

References from The Bookshelf

Ajahn Munindo. (2006). A DHAMMAPADA for Contemplation. Aruna Publications.

Bear, M., & Connors, B. (2015). Neuroscience: Exploring the Brain. Lippineott Williams & Wilkins.

Bodhi, B. (2010). The Noble Eightfold Path: The way to the end of suffering, Kandy: Buddhist Publication Society.

Bhikkhu Bodhi. (2005). In the Buddha's Words: An Anthology of Discourses from the Pali Canon (Teachings of the Buddha). Wisdom Publications.

Coelho, Paulo. (2007). Like a Flowing River; Thoughts and Reflections. HarperCollins Publisher, New Ed edition.

Dr Purushothaman. (2014). What Buddha Said: Selected Sayings & Quotes of Lord Buddha. CreateSpace Independent Publishing Platform.

Gairdames, W., & Kavunatillake, W. S. (1998). A New Course in Reading Pali: Entering the Word of the Buddha. Motilal Banarsidass.

Heads, G. (2017). Living Mindfully: Discovering Authenticity Through Mindfulness Coaching. John Wiley & Sons.

Nelson, Portia. (2018). There's a Hole in My Sidewalk: The Romance of Self-Discovery. Atria Books.

Oliver, Mary. (2004). Wild Geese. Bloodaxe Books; First Edition.

The Dalai Lama., H. C. Cutler. (1999). The Art of Happiness: A Handbook of Living. Hodder Paperbacks.

Thich Nhat Hanh. (2002). No Death, No Fear: Comforting Wisdom for Life. Rider.

Traleg Kyabgon. (2015). Karma: What it is, What is isn't, Why it matters. Shambala.

Walpola Rahula. (1997). What the Buddha Taught. Oneworld Publications.

Watts, A. W. (2008). The Spirit of Zen-A Way of Life, Work and Art in the Far East. Pomona Press.

Weiss, Paul. (2015). Moonlight Leaning Against an Old Rail Fence: Approaching the Dharma as Poetry. North Atlantic Books, U. S.

The Enlightened Spaniel – A Dog's Quest to be a Buddhist (Book 1)

This is the story of a springer spaniel and her half-sister, who set out to discover the reason their owner meditates and is so interested in the teachings of the Buddha. Ably assisted by a bookshelf, who holds a fountain of knowledge, they embark upon a quest to discover the secrets of meditation and uncover the path to ancient wisdom. As they progress along the road to enlightenment, they not only transform their own perception of life, but also the lives of those around them. The journey is a challenging one, but is held together by Half-Sister's wicked sense of humour and a desire to enter into spaniel folklore. The Enlightened Spaniel is a wise tale, filled with insights and humour, that celebrates the connection between all beings that reside on planet earth.

Reviews for the Enlightened Spaniel

An absolutely charming book, it made me laugh and smile as well as being thought provoking. I would highly recommend reading

goodreads

Amazon reviews

I absolutely loved this book! For most of my adult life I have attempted meditation and mindfulness to help me cope with the stresses and strains of modern life. I have never been particularly successful. My own Wandering Mind (explained beautifully and humorously in the book) is a law unto herself! However, if something as scatty as a spaniel can learn to meditate, there's hope for me yet. The book explains the principles of Buddhism in a completely non-dogmatic (no pun intended) way. I am not a Buddhist but agree strongly with the principles which underpin the ethos. I would thoroughly recommend this book to anyone who: wants to learn to meditate more successfully; wants to think about the interconnectedness of all things on this beautiful planet we call home.

Fun to read, and thoroughly uplifting. A complete joy – 5 Stars

This is a lovely tale of 2 Springer Spaniels discovering Buddhism, meditation and mindfulness. All the basics of mindfulness are covered in a thoroughly delightful and funny way as we follow them through their journey of discovery. It is well written and I could almost see Half-Sister sitting in her dignified posture under the bamboo. Definitely a book I will read again.

This book is such a brilliant read. It is a book about Mindfulness written from the point of view of two Springer Spaniels, with such humour. I have found something to laugh out loud to on almost every page. Very cleverly written. I love it.

A beautifully written little book. You don't have to be a dog lover or an aspiring Buddhist, and it definitely makes you laugh, as well as giving a dog's perspective on meditation, mindfulness and other useful practices. Well worth reading and leaves you with a warm glow!

This book is beautiful. Insightful and so well written.

I can relate to the quest for knowledge, and the workings of the Spaniel mind.

Uplifting, funny, wonderful cast of characters.
This book really makes you think.

This book was an unexpected Christmas present from a close friend. It is a beautifully and gently observed tale of two Springers who set out on a mission to learn about Buddhism. You do not have to be a dog lover to enjoy the adventures of Indi and her Half-Sister Ella, but if you know anything about dogs you will often be amused by the apt descriptions of their antics. However, this is not just a tale of canine escapades. It is also an accessible introduction to the philosophy of Buddhism: I find myself drawn to the wisdom it contains. Usually known for rushing through a book, my "Beginner's Mind" is taking this one slowly and appreciating each chapter of the dogs' quest for enlightenment. I have a feeling this will be a treasured and often thumbed addition to my library.

Website
www.garyheads.co.uk
www.rightnuisancepublishing.com

Social Media
Instagram - enlightened_spaniel
Facebook - @EnlightenedSpaniel
Twitter – EnlightSpaniel

In memory of Charlie

I believe cats to be
spirits come to earth.
A cat could, I believe,
walk on a cloud
without falling through.

Jules Verne

Manufactured by Amazon.ca
Bolton, ON

26985769R00122